Cross Trails

Thomas F. Sheehan

Pocol Press
Clifton, VA

POCOL PRESS
Published in the United States of America
by Pocol Press
6023 Pocol Drive
Clifton, VA 20124
www.pocolpress.com

Publisher's Cataloguing-in-Publication

Sheehan, Thomas F. 1928-
    Cross trails / Thomas F. Sheehan.
    pages cm
    ISBN 978-1-929763-66-5

1. Short stories, American. 2. Cowboys--Fiction. 3. Indians of North
America–Fiction. 4. West (U.S.)--Fiction. 5. Western stories. I. Title.

    PS3569.H39216 C76 2015

    813.54 –dc23   2015955681

Library of Congress Control Number: 2015955681

TABLE OF CONTENTS

DEDICATION

I often pause at my writing to bring to mind those who early in their careers wrote in this genre, some who continue to do so, along with hosts of new devotees. They wrote about the cattle, canyons, creeks and cowboys that aided our west-spread growth, much like those B&W giants of old west movies and their seemingly unforgettable "B" type casts, numerous as cattle herds heading for Abilene. They came alive for me in special characterizations. Many were my early heroes, and their type and manly presentations brought a sense of historical reality to an often clumsy fiction we interpreted for joy.

For the forgotten of the lot.

-Thomas F. Sheehan

Great Sky

Nothing showed as splendid and wide as the sky he slept under every night, counting stars, watching the moon develop anew every time out, listening to the ballad and chorus of wolves and coyotes. To him they seemed to enjoy the same grandeur that grabbed him by his boot straps while he dreamed of home beside the river back in Kentucky. Tim Hotchkins, now and then, slept the grandest sleep imaginable. Yet that sleep was full of images, scenes and faces from the past as he moved on his long journey across the middle of America. The one face that stayed the longest, and truest, was his mother's. The Great God above had touched her with a grace he found nowhere else on his journey.

He had spent his last day at home with her and she had commissioned him. In all her grace, and suggestion, she had commissioned him. "We are getting too big for this little corner of a mountain, Timothy. For us there is a place somewhere. Find us some space out there where the land splurges and multiplies under your feet, where grass, I hear, runs for miles and miles like it might be running away from the world itself and right to 'Amen' country. Glory be, when you find the place for us, all of us, let us know. The Good Lord above will let you know. It might happen above you, around you, below you, but you will know."

Her hand on his shoulder touched him with that commission, and a light touch on his face had carried him through clashes with brigands, hostile Indians fighting for their own survival as a people, road agents, women of low intent and high demands. Rock slides and avalanches and wild rivers came his way and he passed by or through them. He had also gone through several lovely places on the road west he thought she would grasp to her bosom. But the high sign had not come to announce any of them.

A matching grace is what he kept looking for on his westward journey.

None of that grace was in Grove City, which he had left the night before, a roaring, glaring new city on the bend of a river rushing out of a rugged mountain setting. A high mountain range he had crossed, wider and higher than the Blue Ridge Mountains, and he came down into the city where the water rushed by on its way out of that range. The river was as fast and as noisy as the city he came into, windows ablaze with night light as he approached the outer edge of small buildings almost sitting in the grass of the prairie, like checkers on the edge of the board. He swore he could not tell the livery from the bank, the structures being identical, but the saloon was the easiest to find, for light was ablaze from half a dozen windows, and also ablaze was the music and noise coming hard as a cavalry charge, drums and bugles to boot, from the saloon as it swept out onto the main road going through the heart of the town.

As always, in the midst of such distractions grabbing at him, he heard the echoes of his mother's voice, her wishes, as though the very breeze carried them from Kentucky and the edge of the mountain back there.

"Count the stars and know the sky when you lay down to sleep, my boy," his mother had said. "When you come to the Great Sky, when you feel it rock through you like a fire of its own and that fire is tended by your happiness, you'll know the place that all the Hotchkins have been waiting a hundred years for. We'll be waiting for the word, come by telegraph, post boy, on the wind, we'll know the place has been found. We'll be counting on you, for you have been born special for this search. I've heard it for forty years; my last born will be the first to find a new home for us. You are my last born and I have waited all this time for your journey. Go with all the good graces I can pray for."

With all that beating at him, knowing the commission of her words, the expectations reigning with it, his throat still knew the dry dust of the open road. That surge of dryness took him toward the lights, the music and the noise.

At the bar of the Golden Palace he was sipping at a mug of beer, mindless of the noise behind him, the sounds of silk and denim at odds and in unison at the same time, when an old gent sauntered to the bar from a corner of the room. His beard was full-blown and white as a puffy cloud, and though tiredness sat on his face, his movements were quicker than one would think. Long life marked itself on his brow and a bulbous scar across his nose the way a bear claw might leave dread intentions.

"Say, son," the old man said, "you appear to me not to be interested in the goings on, but crave on something else. Could you buy a round or two for an old gent who's got the same thirst you have? My name is Calder Willow. I'm a loner."

Hotchkins tapped on the bar loud enough for the barkeep to look at him.

"Set a couple of beers up for Mr. Willow, if you will, and might as well get me another. And I'll make a deal with you, barkeep. You serve me no more than four and then kindly usher me out of this place. That a deal?"

"It would be, except I can't tell the boss that. He'd throw me out as quick. I can appreciate the limit. I can't take too much either, or I'd be starving in a short time."

"I'll make sure of it, son," Willow said, "even if it costs me a few more free drinks. I do appreciate your kindness. Don't always find it less'n

2

you're out on the trail where everybody tends to brotherhood of some sort or other, like giving or taking what suits them. What's your handle and where're you headed?"

"Thanks for the advice, Mr. Willow. Kind voices always have a way of settling on you."

"I wasn't no way wrong about you, son. Not at all. You got goodness on you. I smelt it all across the room like it was honey plugs."

"My name is Tim Hotchkins. Did you ever hear of a place might be called Great Sky or some such?"

Calder Willow, almost old as sin, spun on his boot heels, and stared into Hotchkins' eyes. "Glory be, son, I ain't heard about that place in more than 30 years. Maybe more than 30 years. My father was a mountain man, my mother a Sioux, and he called one place west of here by that very name, Great Sky."

It was Hotchkins' turn to spin on his heels. "You mean there's such a place with that name? Where is it? Far from here? Is it real or imagined most of the way?" Another sip crossed his lips. "You wouldn't be throwing any turd biscuits my way, would you, not an old man like you who's been down the trail?"

"Oh, it's real, son, though it ain't on any map, and there ain't no road sign pointing the way, but I been there and never been able to get back, maybe looking for something else instead, like a damned fool." For a long moment he looked older than he was. In his eyes sat a long look into an unknown past as he stared at the bar top, and perhaps he held his breath a bit longer than he was used to, his face turning pink and flushed around the bushy beard, like it was deliberation itself. And he was politely ignoring, all the while, a salty looking man at the bar leaning their way, intruding like a ferret.

"I can show you the way, if you want me to," Willow said. "Enough twists and turns in the trail to spoil a tracker." The pause was significant in intent, but he did not plead his case. He simply added, "I'd need some grubstaking to get me there. I think the Good Lord might have sent you, for I always meant to get back there but never made it, like I said. Do me that favor, son, and I'll get you to Great Sky. You'll agree with me, and with my Paw, when you see it. It is a dreamland for those who see it 'rightly.'" He stressed the word selection.

"Shucks on me for avoiding it all these years. My Paw said he even stirred up a poke or two of good dust. But I never did see a speck of it, to tell the truth. Man probably lied to get me to stay, but I was burning up with curiosity to see all the other elsewheres."

Hotchkins and old man Willow finished off their appointed rounds at the bar and left the saloon very quietly. Willow, like many old men of wars

3

and battles, kept his eyes on their backside as they headed for the livery where they slept the night at the back of the livery, each telling the other it was a way of saving what money Hotchkins carried. In the morning, in the dawn flash and a big sun promised behind them, the two odd partners set off for Great Sky, westerly, across rivers, to where mountains, as Willow said, "Kiss the clouds on a misty day."

They talked on horseback, as Willow advised they save their mounts as long as they could for "a ride up to the clouds." Often he looked behind them, back down the trail as far as he could see, somewhat sly in his manner.

"Tell me about back home, Tim. Who are the folks back there waiting on your search?" Willow rode almost straight up in the saddle, a little give at his knees, the way age makes demands of the sort. "Besides your mother and paw, who's there?"

"Oh, a passel of us, spread on our corner of the mountain, but we lose ground every time there's a newborn. It's why I'm looking. That's reason enough." His pause was an alert to the old man, who might nod his understanding before words were said, as he did this time, knowing something significant was coming from the young traveler. "My paw went off hunting one day and never came back. We never knew if a bear got him or a mountain lion or some thief looking for a rifle. We never found him or his gun. Part of the reason my mother wants to move, leave the bad memories and get a new start, get us spread out a bit." And in one voice, without changing his tone, said, "What're you looking for behind us all the time?"

"You caught that, eh? 'Member that fellow at the bar, back there at the Golden Palace? He was a might nosy, but he ain't the one behind us. It's a younger feller I just can't get figured yet."

"What do we do about that, turn around and challenge him of a sudden?"

"If he intends to follow us all the way to Great Sky, it's a cinch to nab him, but I ain't sure he's the only one."

"Somebody else? You got good eyes for an old man."

"Yeh," Willow said, "and using them all the way from the saloon and the livery. That nosy feller. He saw some of your money, that I know. Caught his interest in a second, and I suppose he ain't let go yet."

"Can we nab him same as the young fellow?"

"Yep, you do just as I say, and we'll corral both of 'em easy. Great Sky is a great place to grab onto somebody," and he quickly added, "in more ways than one. You'll see that."

For two more days they rode from sunrise into sunset, stopping to water and tend the horses, watching the trail behind them, and seeing

4

nothing of the two trackers. Buzzards added their mysterious flight patterns, as did jack rabbits out on the run of grass. Coyote calls, now and then the scream of a big cat threatening an intruder of a kind, added to the sounds of travel. All the while Willow seemed to follow no landmark trails, but turned now and then in an odd way as if a divine interpretation was at work. It might have been mountain peaks that beckoned him, or the way evening sunlight filtered through passes and canyons setting the route for them.

"Both of them fellers are pretty slick, I'd say," Willow offered a few times, as he studied the trail. "They find what shade and shadow hangs on for the using and make 'em do, as well as the wadis and the arroyos they come across, dipping out of sight for miles. But we'll narrow it all down near Great Sky. Place is meant for selection, if I do say so, and I sure do."

One morning, three days later, Hotchkins awoke from a deep sleep to see in the early haze Willow climbing back to their campsite under a tree on a small hillock in otherwise open ground running along a mountain range. He had no idea where they were.

Willow, slipping back into camp in the haze like a ghost that had been out on a night frolic, said, "Found the second feller back there. It was the feller saw your money at the saloon. He won't be much of a problem; his horse has gone lame on him. I saw nothing of the young one tracking him, but it's like we have one bad one and one good one on our trail. One against the other I'd bet. If the younger feller is a lawman and after the other gent, he could've had him easy by now. And he ain't after us getting away from the law because we ain't broke none." Then he hit Hotchkins with a big surprise: "You any sure that there was no one dogging you since you left home? It's the only thing I can think of."

"Well I never did think of that. You mean maybe since I left home, Ma has snuck someone on my tail?" A huge smile crossed Tim Hotchkins' face. "I wouldn't doubt it one bit. Sounds like something she was bound to do, and if she did, it wouldn't be anybody else but my cousin, Gorman Littlejohn, from the end of the mountain in Kentuck. He's a hunting fool from the first word out of his mouth. Been known to chase down a few thieves, too, that got too frisky around family people. Has the eye and nose of a hound."

"I kind of think that's how he plays the game. Sounds like it's him, from what I've seen of him, and I ain't seen much." He laughed at his own choice of words, tossing his head in a way that pleased Hotchkins with its honesty and joyful celebration.

Later that day, at the foot of a new range of mountain, Willow lead his companion on a torturous trail through rocks, oddly-scarred cliff faces, caves and canyons with so many turns in them, Hotchkins got dizzy thinking about where he had been in the last hours.

At the end of one set of vertical walls in a canyon where the sun never touched one side, Willow took Hotchkins aside and said, "We wait here, behind this stone." It was a huge rock left from a millennium's run into history. "Nobody gets past us now. This is like a jail corridor. We sleep now, and in the morning we'll see Great Sky first hand."

With dawn teasing them the way it does in close quarters, the sound of a pebble rolling on the floor of the canyon woke the two men at once. "Shush," said Willow, pointing. "He's over that way." He retrieved his rifle from his saddle under the overhang and stood to look the way he had pointed. He was unaware of the shadow rising behind him. Their horses snickered in the darkness around the bend.

It was then the shot rang out, a loud echoing blast that ran in the narrow corridor like a train heading down the line. Came to them the sounds of a gasp, a moan, a rifle falling on stone, and the thud of an upright body hitting the rock floor.

All the noise was followed by a yell further behind. "Don't get excited, Cousin Tim. It's me, Cousin Gorman. Your ma sent me as company. This gent had his sights set on one of you. He gets one of you, he gets himself a horse. His animal ain't much good now. Damned fool left his horse to die. That surely made me angry. I had to put the critter down. No man ought to do that to his horse."

The introductions were made, and Calder Willow said, "We might as well finish this journey today. We put this bushwhacker in a proper setting, say our prayers for his soul, and find what a great chunk of Kentucky's been looking for."

Several hours later the trio came out of a tight squeeze through a maze of rock walls and a cave as big as a ranch house. They came out on the higher lip of a full-flung valley that ran for miles in the basket of mountains around it. The grass was as green as ever seen, a small waterfall poured itself off a mountain face in a continuing gesture of earth's richness, the leaves of timberland trees covered one whole side of a mountain until it ran out of sight against the stone peak, and overhead, in a display of god-given grandeur the heavens glowed with a high blue of uncountable grace that stunned all three men, including the man who had seen it all before, and wondered again why he had ever left it.

A Mannequin for Missy Drumm

Every good morning the sun sat like a flame in the window of Missy Drumm's women's store in Wallow Creek, Wyoming. She went outside early each day to see that window display for herself, from where her customers could see it and warm up to a purchase as they came into town on errands, visits or head off to jobs. Since the day the store opened she felt the scene was incomplete for some reason. The store was a gift on her 21st birthday from her father, Caleb Drumm, exactly one month before he was killed by an unknown person out on the road to town from his ranch. He had requested her not to go into town until he said it was okay, her knowing all the while that he was planning something special for her birthday coming along.

The first thing she saw on that birthday was the sign over the front entrance, "Missy Drumm's Ladies Apparel." Her mother, gone a half dozen years, would have loved it too, she told herself. Missy remembered how her mother would drape a sheet of fabric on her fashioning a new dress, a blouse, a skirt, her father across the large kitchen smiling at his pair of designers.

Missy was Caleb Drumm's only child and no further information surfaced on his death for a whole year. In that time a number of beaus and prospective suitors had in some way meandered or squeezed into the scene, and none made any headway. Missy would be a good catch for any man, owning the ranch of decent size, and the store, which had been a dream of hers for a long time. In one sense she had relaxed into her duties at the store, leaving the ranch to be run by an old friend of her father's, Hoke Willett, sometimes irascible but faithful to his last breath. And the alter-father figure for Missy.

Though not apparent to her friends and customers, she continually eyed the horizon for the secret kindred soul to enter her life, to make it complete. But the death of her father hung in the way of all prospects.

One young man, Charlie deRochemont, son of a small rancher some ways up the valley, never once approached Missy after her father's death, but had danced with her once years earlier at a barn raising; he had not forgotten the experience. He appeared to all as a hard-working and pleasant young man with a fair complexion despite his work habits, stood almost six-feet tall and looked much taller in a Stetson that had a curved brim, laughed easily at jokes and at himself when he was the object of a joke or a prank, made proper restitution at his own speed, and seemed promised to leave the single life when he passed into his 30th year … but having no firm prospect.

So, the way fate moves sometimes, slow as a drying stream, or fast as a stampede, young deRochemont, in a distant town at the end of a drive, sat watching a poker game in a saloon as he and other drovers celebrated the finish of their task. His eyes kept moving back to one of the players, a mustached man with a small Van Dyke at the tip of his chin, quick hands that bespoke dexterity in most situations, and a pair of eyes that missed nothing of the game … or in the room about him. He had noticed deRochemont staring at him a few times, discounted the stares as coming from his three straight wins of good-sized pots. Only when he lost three hands in a row, and the young man kept staring at him, gambler and card man Chet Durwood asked deRochemont if he wanted to sit in.

"You look like you have interest, son. Am I right?"

"Naw," deRochemont replied, "I just think I saw you play before, maybe over in Jerry's Caves," which was a town much further away from this town and well away from Wallow Creek.

Durwood sat back satisfied. He had no idea he had exposed some trait or some fact that deRochemont had seized and kept adjusting in his mind, putting things in place.

Young deRochemont, with a sudden inspiration, as if on quick thought, said, "Yeh, why not. I'll sit in." He took a fold of bills from his pocket and sat at the table. The move surprised a few of his old friends who had never seen him gamble before. They were not surprised when Charlie deRochemont lost his whole share from the drive in a matter of a few hands, betting crazily and steadily without a decent set of cards.

When all his money was lost, deRochemont stood up and said, "I'd like another shot at you, mister. When I get back home and get some more money, I'll try to get back my losses. Where will I find you? Will you still be here?"

"In this business, son, you have to keep moving. I'm heading up to Fernville next and Wampus after that, seeing some old friends and my sister I haven't seen in a few years. I'd be pleased to see you again." He paused, reflected, and said, "Chet Durwood's the name and poker's my game."

He waved off deRochemont as if he had not existed, and went right back to his game as another sucker sat in.

Charlie deRochemont left town and headed back home, knowing Durwood's vanity had gotten the upper hand in the game.

He went directly to see Missy Drumm at her store.

Two days later, the pair, with Hoke Willett in tow as if he was a chaperone, headed for Wampus. On the long ride that took several hours, Missy kept stealing looks at Charlie deRochemont. Her smiles were hidden, she thought, though Hoke Willett, too many times around the corral, kept nodding his assessment and his appreciation of the young pair.

A number of times, so many that deRochemont thought Missy might be finding doubts, she asked, "Are you sure, Charlie? Are you really sure? I can't believe it, after all this time."

"I'm as positive as I've ever been about anything in my life, except one other thing."

"What is that, Charlie?" she said, her interest piqued again by the young man who rode so easily in the saddle.

"Maybe I'll get to tell you sometime," he said.

Hoke Willett never missed a word of their talk, including the interests and aspirations, and with deRochemont's description of the gambler Durwood set in his mind, went into the second saloon in Wampus and saw the gambler engaged in a game with three cowpokes. The cards in Durwood's hands flew with ease, the smooth noise of shuffling a distraction unto itself. And as advised by deRochemont, he noticed other things about the man as he kept up a series of winning two or three times in every four or five pots, but always the best pots.

In the corner of the saloon, in the shadows where he spent most of his adult life, a protector, a watchdog over the likes of Missy Drumm, willing ever to step over the line when needed, Willet knew he was in contrast to the young deRochemont, not as eager but as sure, not as quick as he once was but lethal all the same, all the while keeping Missy's best comfort in mind.

With an age-old comfort, he measured the gambler, noted his actions, saw the distorted "Ds" but still "Ds" on the holsters Durwood wore on his gun belt. The holsters were not those of Caleb Drumm, but the two "Ds", hammered a bit to disfigure them somewhat, had been fired up on the Drumm ranch for the boss himself. There was not a single doubt in Hoke Willet's mind, as there had been none in Charlie deRochemont's mind.

They were probably being worn by Caleb Drumm's killer, who had stolen much of his personal gear at the scene of the crime.

The three sleuths gathered in a small café to discuss their plans.

Missy said, "I'd like to run in there and shoot him now, but I know you're right about him maybe finding or buying those Drumm "Ds" that were my father's. How do we prove it?"

Willett said, "If we can get him to say he bought them or had them made up, we can trace back to who he says sold them to him. If he says he had them made, we know he's lying and can get the sheriff in on it."

"How do we do that?" Missy said. "All he does is play cards from what's said about him."

Hoke Willett said, "We use a card game to get him strung out, and use his strength against him."

9

Missy, alarmed, totally transparent in her response, said, "You don't want Charlie in a game with that killer, do you, Hoke?" Her hand reached and covered deRochemont hand on the table. It had confirmed all that Willett had wished for in the pair.

"No way, Missy. This old man here will get in a game with him and twist him just the right way. All I want him to say is that he had those "Ds" made special, then I'd duel him myself if it came down to that. Your father kept me on through the lean years. It'd be payback time, I figure." There was a distant look in his eyes, as if debts had already been cleared, restitution made. "You two stay outside until this is all over. I don't want either one of you getting hurt, and I'm counting on that."

His voice changed. Missy had not heard that new tone before when he said, "Hear me?" His eyes made the punctuation too, as the old friend asserted his control.

In the saloon, Willett eyed Durwood's every move, saw him win more than he lost, drive poorer and less skilled players right out of the game. The man's hands were as slick as any Willett had ever seen, and he had every belief that his gun hand was just as skillful. Yet a sliver of an idea seemed to lean out of Willett's intelligence, trying to be known. At first he fought it, then saw it and realized it, and abruptly left the saloon, but not without saying to the whole saloon in general and to Durwood in particular, "That man sure has a ton of luck hanging around him. Before I sit down with him for a game I'm off to the old sachem of the hill tribe to catch onto some of that luck. The old Injun up there in the hills said I could come by anytime and get some more. I tell you, gents, it's got me this far in life." His hand waved in the air as he added, "Them Injuns got something we ain't found yet."

There was a roll of laughter that ran clear through the saloon as Willett stepped outside the swinging doors.

Caleb Drumm's favored ranch hand, and protector of the boss's daughter, lit out of town, telling Missy and Charlie deRochemont he'd be back in a few hours, and for them to "Stay clear of that gambler in there." He nodded at the saloon as he left them.

In a matter of an hour he was back, entered the saloon, flashed a wad of money, and stumbled as he sat beside Durwood in a vacant chair. The stumbling move was a cover for his affixing to the "D" on Durwood's holster a rather small and crude object that immediately clung to the iron "D." it was a piece of cobalt and iron that had come out of Canada a long time ago, and was fully magnetic.

Willet didn't doubt that the magnetic pull would slow the draw of the weapon in the holster.

And he'd have to wait for the right moment.

He didn't see Charlie deRochemont enter the saloon and stand at the far end of the bar.

When Willett saw the move he was waiting for, he challenged Durwood to produce the Jack he had discarded from his hand. "I saw that move with my Jack, mister. You're cheating and I want my money back."

Everything happened in a hurry.

Durwood went for his weapon.

Willett went for his.

One of Durwood's cronies, elsewhere in the room, went for his weapon. He happened to be too near Charlie deRochemont who knocked the gun out of his hand.

"Another stupid move like that, Mister," deRochemont said, "and you won't believe what'll happen to you." A gun was stuck into the man's side.

Meanwhile, called out in the open, exposed as a cheat, Durwood's draw was slow. He had difficulty in getting his gun from his holster with his usual speed, something strange slowing down his draw.

Willett's gun was on Durwood, and the old man said, "Tell us where you bought those "Ds" on your holsters, or where you had them made."

The gambler, and the killer, suddenly knew he was exposed as a killer also. Flustered, realization hitting him, he finally told his entrapping lie, "I had a man make them, from over at Dunphy way. He's an iron man."

"You're a liar, Durwood. You stole them from Caleb Drumm when you bushwhacked him on the trail a whole year ago and stole his gear. Those "Ds" were made right on his ranch."

The hunk of Indian cobalt and iron that had come out of Canada a long time ago with the old Injun sachem, also full of a spiritual magnetism, still clung to the iron "D" on Durwood's holster.

And Charlie deRochemont, an observant and thoughtful young man, also fully aware for a long time of a lack in Missy Drumm's store window display, ordered a dress maker's mannequin for his betrothed all the way from St. Louis.

Hooligan Hide-out

The trap, without the slightest hint obvious, was already set, and Kate Osgood, studying one strange and suspicious rider, was in turn studied by another rider she did not know, behind her, above her.

Kate Osgood, on her red sorrel on one rim of Los Gatos Canyon, stared down at the floor of the canyon studying the lone rider roaming the area as if lost. Or, came a second thought, as if he was searching for the secret exit from Spider's Valley, location of the Kay-Bar-Kay Ranch, her home for the past 15 years. The ranch, and the valley, was now hers since her father had been killed, in error, by a misguided posse just a few weeks earlier.

The rider had discerning traits and character moves that she'd be able to pick out later on, by her system of personal identity that was pretty solid. Kate would know him arriving in town, riding lead or drag on a drive, approaching her at the ranch on horseback with flowers in his hand. On a classic paint, the horseman rode with one shoulder somewhat ahead of the other, the right, as though he'd be looking behind him so often it was best to be part ways there all the time. He exhibited that tendency a number of times in his search.

When the rider kept the reins in his right hand, she assumed him to be a lefty, the left hand ready to draw his weapon if needed.

"This one's a lefty, Joe," she said to her horse, "so remember that." She patted him in a salute of trust and loyalty. "Oh, good horse, I wonder what Toby Booker would say about him, if he'd look at him like we do?" The subsequent smile gleamed on her face as the rider took off his hat and scratched his head. Toby, she'd quickly admit, was not a second thought type of acquaintance. Her only question, never having seen him in action, was would he be able to handle some normal adversity. Heaven knows, there was enough of it floating about. You could stab it with a jack knife if you were at all alert to the full life going on in this part of the country.

The rider seemed in a quandary, as if he could not find the exit from the valley ... meaning, she realized, he might have been here before, one of the various intruders over the years who had might have slipped from the valley strictly by accident or in a desperate flight from the law ... or who might have been escorted pronto from the ranch property by her father.

Suddenly, Kate's suspicion was aroused as the thought hit home, and she shifted into anger. Why was the world like this, its people scrounging around for a dead man's property, trying to exercise new rights over old land, trying for easy pickings from a girl? She slapped the pistol at her side in a determined reaction. This was her heritage, her legacy. She'd fight to keep it that way. The rumors floating all about town and across the grass to some of the other ranches had bothered her from the first day. They loomed so unfair, the cheaters lining up to grab from a supposedly helpless girl her birthright, the choicest valley in the whole mountain chain. Nothing else measured up to it.

Back in the beginning, her father knew the value of the valley the moment he saw it unfold before him, his mule on its last legs, his water gone and his ammunition spent. His spirits had shortly before fallen downhill so fast he feared he'd never get back to the wagon where Kate and her mother were hidden in a small dead end canyon a few miles away. He had arrived here through a maze of rocks and mountain fissures cracked open by Mother Nature in an escarpment that rose more than 500 feet, like the side of a huge barn. The way proved to be the door to Utopia.

Life had changed in one look, for at that exact minute a spider slipped down past his eyes on a gossamer thread to land on his sleeve, and so he called the place Spider's Valley.

This was her land, Spider's Valley. She would keep it until her last breath. She slapped the sidearm again. "It won't be easy, Mister," she said aloud, the words coming from her mouth with the depths of an oath.

Kate knew that if the strange rider found the secret exit from Spider's Valley, she could come in behind him from another direction. This was part of her father's precautions to insure the safety of the family, a tunnel of sorts. The tunnel, through a thousand years of falling rocks, landslides, eruptions of cataclysmic sorts, had opened up for him with one stick of dynamite all those years earlier. After many trips into and out of the tunnel, Kate could pass through it with a blindfold in place. And her father had placed a few caches of other insurances within the tunnel, Kate being the only other person in Creation ever to know the secret locations of weapons, ammunition and sundry supplies.

Time, fate, and what else could expose the glories of Spider's Valley might now be upon her. For a long time she had dreaded a run of people into the valley, the existence of its choice location admired by many people, people who rarely came without invitation and guidance. There were those, Kate realized, who would adapt the place as a hide-out with a built-in escape route known to nobody else, if they ever found that route. Discourage the sternest lawmen, it would. The valley was surrounded on just about every side by high rises of the lofty Rockies, and would naturally bar all but the direct approach by the "front door," as her father would always say about visitors.

The fates and the accidents were merging to drop their big surprise on the young mistress of Spider's Valley. The rider below, with a seeming mild curiosity, dismounted and went behind a huge stone slab and Kate

13

knew the secret was exposed. The rider came back for his horse, mounted again and disappeared behind the rock. He would follow the opening into the valley. She then slipped carefully into the tunnel, unaware of the second man watching her movements from above.

Kate's suspicions, of course, were right in line, but she had no idea to the depth of the plans to take over her homestead.

Things, all adverse to her good cheer and comfort, happened rapidly. As she came out of a fissure in the mountain, the rider was directly in front of her. He was a lefty, she saw, with a revolver on his left hip. Her rifle was pointed right at him as she slowly came up behind him and said, "You're trespassing, Mister, so I'm chasing you out of here. You keep your hand away from your gun and ride right down the valley and out the other end. I don't know what you're doing here, but it's all over as of now."

The stranger, wide at the shoulders, thick and immoveable at the jaw, and not fazed a bit by her rifle aimed at his mid-section, said, "Sorry about this, lady, but we got too many plans for this place. This is going to be our new hide-out, and there's not a lot you can do to stop us. We got guys all over you and all over this place. You're gonna keep house for us, that's for sure."

Kate studied him. "I could shoot you right now, knock you right out of your saddle, couldn't I?"

"Then we'd have the place without any problems, wouldn't we?" He pressed his lips together, nodded and added, "Doesn't that bother you at all, us moving in just the way the boss planned it?"

"How'd you ever find the way in to the valley?"

"The boss left here one day after visiting your father, saying he was going off to see his folks back down the river, but met his dad on the way. When he got to town with his father, your father had been in town for almost two hours. He knew there had to be a way out of the valley that nobody else knew about, the way your father got to town in such a hurry. The boss figures this'd be a great place for a hide-out with a way out just in case we needed it. Made to order, he says, and he knows his way around."

"Who's your boss?" Kate said, as an unnerving and intolerable thought came to her.

"Oh, you're sure to meet up with him doing all the housekeeping he'll make you do to keep us comfortable. He's got it all figured out. That's why he's the boss, but you wouldn't know it meeting him the first time around."

That sick feeling Kate had felt but a moment earlier came back with a vengeance. She ought to shoot this intruder to get ahead of them, whoever "they" were. Her rifle was pointed with authority at the intruder, but Kate Osgood couldn't pull the trigger. She had never shot at a man before;

14

hadn't much as aimed her rifle at a man in all her 20 years. She tried to remember if there were any times that she had threatened to shoot a man, but nothing of the sort came back from her past. Everything wrong in her life was right here in front of her … an intruder had found his way into the valley, a false friend had intruded earlier, and her father was dead, supposedly by an ill-advised posse. She wondered about that, felt it all piling up on her.

Everything in the world was wrong.

Yet it was the other sound that commanded her attention, the click of a trigger being cocked on a weapon. A voice behind her, another but deeper voice, more threat in it, said, "Don't try it, Missy, or your ranching days are over."

Kate Osgood did not even turn around. Realization swiftly told her the tunnel had been breached in her anxiety to trap the first intruder. She had dropped her guard, had let herself be caught, and somebody from town, some acquaintance of hers, some friend of her father's, was behind it all. She had to know who it was.

She dropped her rifle.

But she didn't panic. Thoughts of her father filled her, his early and steady precautions for his family, and it would be up to her to avail herself of them at an opportune time. Obviously it was not now. More than her own safety bothered her; her curiosity was aroused to a compelling level. Who had cheated her father? Who had cheated her in turn? Who would pay for all this? The eventual pay-back aroused ferocity in her soul she had not known before.

She'd keep her mouth shut, her eyes open, and do what she was told.

There was a way out of all this. Did her father see all of this coming?

With reins not in her hands, Kate Osgood was lead to the door of her home. The flowers she had picked on the prairie sat in a pot at the front steps, a dozen blossomed flowers with long stems and their dozen hues waved in any breath of air … someone walking in or out, the door opened to cause a draft of air, a hand reaching for the welcome touch of nature. They sat proper as daylight in an old Canopic jar she had found in the mountains. She had spent a few hours at the task of gathering, selecting, and arranging them in their variety of colors. She loved the sight of the blossoms showing against the dark wall of the house. Aromas reached her as she arrived at the hitch rail. She stared at two flowers boxes, brilliant in half a dozen hues, sitting tight against the wall on each side of the door, at the same level of the doorknob. Her personal statements were open and readable, by most visitors, by all guests. Everything said care and comfort abounded at the Kay-Bar-Kay Ranch in Spider's Valley.

Now it was a lie.

Even in their brightness, the splash of colors from the flowers paled as she dismounted. Home suddenly felt foreign, strange in a false welcome, as though nothing would ever be the same again; a time had passed; another time was coming, and it disheartened Kate for a short while, until her spirit, always with her, found resurrection, leaped with this discovery as though it was new.

The man who had come in from behind her at the tunnel escorted into the house, holding her roughly by the elbow at first. "You better get busy in the kitchen, Lady, 'cause the boss'll want something to eat when he shows up. He'll be here sooner than you think. Best to feed him quick afore he gets real angry. I don't want him any none angry at me, I'll tell you."

He pushed her toward the kitchen, his hand lingering too long at her backside. She shuddered.

For sanity's sake, Kate immediately pictured the cached goods in the tunnel; the images saved her from panic once and would do so again. Now she called them up for visual assurance as she heard hoof beats coming in from the valley opening. That she might know the boss of the gang filled her with dread; life couldn't be any more unfair than it was now. Up with a quick start she came; the only recent guest she could remember coming to the ranch was Toby Booker. That such a mild, unaggressive man could have planned all this, played his charade to perfection, was unthinkable to her. But now she'd know what a fool she had been to hold any secret desires about Toby. Love was so damned foolish, she believed, as if her pain had falsely blossomed into love by the quick absence of its possibility. She was stupid to have held a single dream, or any such idea, of Toby Booker. Anger moved again in her blood as the door opened.

A breath escaped her lungs. Her heart dropped and then leaped in her chest. It was not Toby Booker. It was not Toby Booker! How had she been so frail in her thinking? Toby didn't deserve any of it. The man standing in the doorway, tall, soft in the face as though he had been beaten down by something, his shoulders sloped and hardly discernable in a gray shirt and a black vest, was a man she had seen before, but always on the edges in town, like a ferret, a malingerer, a malcontent uncomfortable alone or in a crowd. The only thing that saved his presence was the stolen, molten blue of his eyes looking at her without a bit of anger or shame. They were eyes that could measure things generally unseen, that could reach down into her soul and expose her thoughts, her intentions, enforce demands.

"I'm going to say this to you once, Fancy Lady … I'll kill the first person who comes to the ranch and you try to give them any messages or cry for help. You're now working for me, and I'm damned hungry. You get something to eat for me and a few of the boys, all my boys. Your small crew was taken care of while you were prancing around the country like

16

you owned it all. No more, Fancy Lady, no more. One of us will be sitting with you as we go about your business here and our business out in the world of finances." Distastefully, he emitted a vulgar chuckle from deep in his throat as though it was being scraped across a corrugated board.

Kate, pride and thanks in hand, swallowed a whole lot, took deep her thanks that it was not Toby Booker making demands on her. She'd have some freedom of movement about the ranch as long as she stayed alert for an escape attempt. Sometime, with patience and planning her father was so good at, she'd make a move to reach arms, find help, get rid of the reins holding her in place, perhaps say some words to Toby that had long gone unsaid. She hoped that she would say the right things in the right way, that rescue would not make word choices for her. She wondered how she really felt. Toby Booker on a white horse did not come into her mind; another comfort found its way.

For three weeks, with a shepherd along every minute, Kate Osgood moved within the closed bounds of the Kay-Bar-Kay Ranch as the gang of hoodlums and hooligans went out and came back on following days. Loud talk filled in the description of their days; two stage hold-ups, a bank robbery, one former member of the gang, telling tales, ambushed on a lonely trail, his mouth shut forever.

At the end of that third week a rider came into the valley and rode up to the hitch rail. It was a friendly ranch hand passing by who wanted to say hello. She heard him talking to one of the gang. "Would you tell Kate that Joel Haggland wants to say hello. I'm just passing by. My sister said to say hello too." And realizing he was talking to a new hired hand, he said, "You're a new hand, ain't cha? Ain't seen you afore."

"Yep. I came on a few weeks ago when some of the boys just up and finally rode off after the old gent got killed. Like they didn't want to work for no woman boss. I'll get Kate for you, but she ain't been feelin' too good the last few days. You best wait here."

Kate's shepherd came into the house and said, "There's a fella name of Haggland wants to say hello. Take care what you say or the boss, over in the barn, will drop him right off'n his saddle. You got his life in your hands now, so do what the boss says. It's easy for you, I bet."

Kate went out to the porch and said, "I'm glad you came by to say hello, Joel, but I've been feeling poorly lately. I know your sister wants to come by sometime. Just tell her I'll let her know when I'm feeling better. And tell Toby too." She saw movement at the barn door and continued, "I do feel poorly, Joel. I better go inside and rest. I'll see you another time. I'm sorry about this."

She turned around, walked slowly into the house and closed the door behind her. From a window she saw Haggland sit his saddle and ride away

17

from the ranch.

All was quiet. Her breath came back slowly with the silence. Haggland turned onto the trail to town and went out of sight.

Control of her nerves seemed sufficient to get her through the following days, just as they had for the three past weeks. It was nighttime when the frayed edges worked a bit of trouble, waiting for the door to her room to open in the middle of the night. That never happened.

Two more expeditions left the camp and the gang was gone for two days on one trip and one day on another trip. They began drinking heavily at night after the second trip and she knew another bank had been robbed successfully. All the bragging and descriptions of the robbery came audibly to her room where she slept fully clothed every night. The noise level rose, the drinking got louder, and then silence descended as night crawled into the next day.

The squeak at the door sent a tingle down her backside. Kate fished for the horseshoe hidden under her pillow. Her hand circled a grip on one end of the iron shoe. The floor also sounded the tread of weight as it whispered a protest. A hand was touching her leg under the blanket. The smell of whiskey came close to her face. Too close to her face. With all her might she swung the horseshoe at the smell and caught the intruder flush on the temple. He collapsed with a groan onto the edge of the bed and slipped to the floor.

Her heart was in her throat. She listened for action. The silence continued, then loud snoring from the rest of the house. The intruder, of course, was not wearing a gun belt. She took two belts from her rack and bound his hands and legs and stuffed a kerchief in his mouth. Wearing moccasins and a light jacket, Kate Osgood slipped out her bedroom window and made her way toward the tunnel. She did not go near the horses fearing their noise would wake up one of the gang; she'd have to walk, hoping to meet somebody on horseback or in a wagon. Perhaps a stagecoach on the river road or a freighter's wagon. Her mind leapt with possibilities.

In 15 minutes she was in the tunnel and unearthing the supplies she needed. God bless her father! A gun belt and a handgun in a holster fit snuggly on her waist. A rifle and two boxes of shells came out of a blanket and canvas that had been set deep into a niche well off the ground. From a deeper and tighter niche she withdrew a few sticks of dynamite.

"You thought of everything, Pa." The tears came to her eyes in the darkness. "I know they had something to do with killing you, Pa," she said slowly, "so we'll take care of them right proper. I don't know what happened to our ranch hands, but somehow we'll find out about that too."

Two sticks of dynamite received an extra steady insertion into a

18

crevice no bigger than her wrist. It was a critical point in the tunnel, at a spot where her father had spelled out specific instructions. The wall of rock about her seemed to tremble as the dynamite was placed between two solid surfaces.

"A sign of things to come," she muttered to herself and to the whole of justifiable Creation, as she patted the stone slabs. A giddy sense of achievement slid into her being, which she shrugged off as too early for a celebration. The caution came as a full alert: this was her only chance and she better make sure of each step and not get too far ahead of herself. There was no telling what they'd do to her if things went awry.

The rock slabs were patted again, as if she sent good luck their way.

"This'll break bones, Pa," she said aloud, "and shake the mountain to pieces, I swear." A savage joy tickled Kate Osgood for a moment; she felt it all the way down to her toes snuggled in the moccasins. Her imagination was lit up as lightning and thunder and earthly cataclysm echoed and vibrated with the arm of justice doing its promised work. Getting even could be as sweet as an early blossom in the snow or a cool sarsaparilla on the hottest day of the year.

The giddiness came again.

Kate positioned herself by the escape route and aimed her rifle into the narrow aperture, just as shadows of night began to play tag with false dawn. The gang members could only come one at a time, never two abreast, never two guns against her one rifle. As directed so long ago, she lit the fuse that would blast the tunnel into a solid impasse, and hefted her rifle to take on any of the gang who might try the escape route.

She watched the sparks of the fuse as it crawled toward the tunnel, about 30 feet from her position. Breath seemed to hold itself in her chest.

The whole Earth did not explode, to her surprise. There was a mere thud, a meager bumping of the Earth. Then a slow rush of sound. A cloud of dust. And only then, beneath her feet, did the mountain shake.

It was a dull revelation. She was convinced, however, that the tunnel was blocked and she'd now have to contend with gang members trying the escape route. They'd know she had set off a blast to cut down one route.

Behind her, totally unsuspected, came another sound; spurs touching rock, a man walking, a voice saying, "Who's there? Who are you? Speak up."

It was the voice of Toby Booker. It rang in her.

"Toby, that's you, isn't it? Oh, my, you came right in time. Right in time." The giddy feeling came back. Something else was with it. She wished she could see Toby's face. Only parts of it flashed in her mind.

"My gosh, Kate, what's going on in there? I knew something was wrong when Joel told me what he saw, what he knew, that you were sick and your old hands had all run off on you. I know no one would do that, Kate. Not one of those boys would leave you like that. Your pa took care of that a long time ago."

"Why are you here, Toby?"

"Joel knew something was wrong, but he couldn't say what. He had a feeling, and so did I. I've been here for two days. Came out a few other times, but was careful. I always knew about the escape your pa had found from the valley. The sheriff and the posse will be at the other end either today or tomorrow. I told him I could hold off an army at this end for a week if I had to. I've been in and out of there half a dozen times. Even saw you one time the way they were treating you, but I had to convince the sheriff he ought to do something. So he's on the other side and I'm at this end, waiting. Like I said, been here almost two days this trip. We know it's a hooligan gang been doing lots of hold-ups."

Catching his breath, obviously happy to know she was okay, Toby declared, "Nobody knows what happened to your crew, Kate. Not a word. Sheriff fears the worst. We might never find out. What was that sound I heard a little while ago?"

"I set off a couple of sticks of dynamite to block off a second way out of the valley. My pa had it set up all these years. Kept it right up to snuff, he did. You ready for company, Toby? They'll be coming our way soon."

"One at a time, Kate," Toby said. "That's all they can do. We got them covered, you and me, Kate Osgood and Toby Booker. What a pair."

Kate Osgood figured Toby Booker was smiling in the dark and she knew the tingles again.

Fair Exchange

When Marshal Max Preshong walked into the biggest saloon in Waco, after being out on a posse for almost three days successfully chasing down a rustler and killer, a small man, not a cow man, slipped out the side door. Nobody saw him leave except Max Preshong. From outside the door for a short time he had noticed the man sitting alone at a corner table studying every man in the room, every new-comer, all the while playing make-believe with a deck of cards, waiting. Preshong was sure the man was waiting for him, waiting to scramble and tell someone that the marshal was back in town.

Who might that be, waiting such information? He wondered for but a second and slipped back out the front door and saw the scrambler entering the hotel. Outside Preshong stayed in the shadows across the road and watched the windows, saw a shade drawn, a light go on inside, had his man.

The hotel register said "Blare Fenton, ST Co." The name was printed in a bold and stumpy fashion, like a man who had trouble formulating the words, was copying words from another paper, was just learning to write, or was missing fingers on his writing hand.

There! He had it. Butch Fallon on the loose again, and, as usual, paving his way for a new activity, laying groundwork, keeping a schedule on the local law. Butch Fallon, once a righty with his six guns, now a lefty, with right-hand two fingers displaced by one shot from Preshong all of ten years earlier, and his eventual stay behind bars for eight years.

Preshong pushed through his mind the possible target in Waco that Fallon might have interest in. There was a lot going on in the burgeoning town; the Chisholm Trail crossed the Brazos River here at Waco, the new bridge over the Brazos was now open to wagon traffic, horsemen and those who came by foot because of one circumstance or another. Some of those pedestrians had been robbed of their wagons or horses, and all their valuables taken. In addition, the tracks for The Waco and Northwest Railroad had arrived and the fertility of the Brazos Valley gave significant promise to agriculture. With all business on an upswing, the banks were active.

"Rustling isn't my only problem," Preshong said to himself as he kept his eye on the hotel window where he was sure Fallon was accepting the information that the marshal was back in town. He tried to separate all the opportunities for theft that had surfaced within Waco as business had developed. Rustling, he might have said, was a lot of work, and now, that it was not the only target, he'd have to agree that the banks or a rail car were prime objectives for easy money … but he was a major deterrent to that kind of activity. He and Fallon, and any other worldly robber newly arrived in Waco or the vicinity of the Brazos Valley, had to know that. His reputation was widespread; in a battle he was as good as his gun; in criminal detection, he was at least a day ahead of those who intended to thwart him or his constituents.

"Whatever he's planning, he needs me out of the way," he said in a soft whisper, still keeping himself in the dark recess where he had in view the upstairs window and the front entrance. "So, it's going to be a bushwhacking most likely, something coming from false information or a phony cry for help. All the possibilities raced through his mind. Each one was clicked into his memory, filed away, an alert being built into his mind; a gunshot from darkness, a cry for help from a woman most likely, an unknown rider reporting a bad incident outside of town, perhaps a body in the road, a ranch house burning, a stampede of an arriving herd. Along with each particular thought came an image … he had the ability to "see" how something would take place, how it would act out with certain characters, what had really taken place to foment the alarm.

Now he brought those summoning powers into force, all based on knowledge already in place, his knowing who he was dealing with or would have to deal with. That is how the scene would develop behind the window he was looking at, the soft glow shimmering at the edges from a candle or an oil lamp, the two men facing each other in the mere light. He was sure of it: the scrambler would have his hand out for money, for his pay-off for the information provided; Fallon would search in his pockets for a likely sum and turn it over to the scrambler. There would be a stern admonishment from Fallon about divulging any of the transaction, a threat as heavy as silence could make it, as simple as a nod at his gun hanging by the bed in a well-worn holster, a shake of the head, a "No" unsaid on his lips, but heard just the same.

The scrambler would nod his silent agreement and leave the room. Preshong swore he could hear the steps on the stairs. Within seconds the scrambler came out the hotel door and disappeared down a side alley; he was now out of the picture.

Fallon, the pursuer, was now the pursued. Preshong stepped further into is dark recess. He'd stay awake for 48 hours if need be. But he was sure it would not take long.

It didn't.

Ten minutes later the fragile light behind the window curtain went out. Two or three minutes later, sly as a lead scout, Fallon came out the hotel door, crossed the road at an oblique angle, headed straight for one of the town's three liveries. In another ten minutes he rode slowly out of town, heading north. It was just after midnight. Preshong stayed in the depths of the shadows for almost half an hour. Street traffic was light. A few drunks announced themselves at odd moments. A carriage rolled softly into town and parked in front of one of the small town houses further down the road. He suspected it was one of the two doctors returning from a late call. His dog welcomed him home; there was indistinguishable chatter, body noises.

In a quarter of an hour, he figured, he headed north out of town, his horse at an easy walk. A filigree moon peaked through clouds just as thin. A barn owl stated his position in the night. A dog, locked inside one of the buildings at the edge of town, whined his disposition. Preshong noticed and accepted it all, just parts of his day. Things, for the time being, were normal and were to be enjoyed. It was the way they were.

So as not to get caught up in euphoria, he sent his summoning powers ahead of him; Fallon, believing he was alone on the road, or at least having nobody knowing what he was up to, would keep his journey as shadowy and as silent as possible. There'd be no hurry, no galloping, no noise. He'd have at least five hours of darkness to get his plan into action. The less he was noticed, the better off he'd be, and the surer was the outcome. That was all the caution he used.

When he left the road and moseyed up into a small canyon in the foothills sweeping down to the Brazos, he did not even take a look behind him in the darkness. The smell of pinion smoke sifted down to him, and then the aroma of coffee; they'd be waiting for him.

Marshal Max Preshong was half an hour away from those smells, those canyon signals, his horse keeping at a slow gait, then, closing down distance and time, he thought, "Hell, I hope there's enough coffee to go around."

In a clutch of brush at the edge of the canyon he tethered the horse, slipped his rifle from the saddle, and walked slowly and quietly to find a hummock where he could survey the area. The sound of horses at a stand came to him, slight snickers, in the far night a wolf howled. From an old line cabin he knew to be long out of general use, he saw a glow of light. He lay down to watch, and wait. The grass was soft and thick and he knew practically anything could grow along the Brazos. The smell of green things also came to him, and then an image. It was associated with a small red flicker, off to one side of the cabin; a lookout on watch, his cigar or cigarette sighting his position. The small illumination lasted for almost five minutes ... but did not move. The lookout was stationary, he thought, possibly tired, sleepy, and not fully alert.

Preshong got really close to the spot. He could see the slump in the lookout's posture. When he said, in a decidedly sincere voice, "Move and you're dead," there was no response except the sound of a rifle sliding down to the ground, the lookout standing, saying, "That you, Marshal? I tried to get them to know who we'd have to buck for this job, but they don't know of you like I've heard."

"Who are you," Preshong said, "and who's inside the cabin? How many? What's Fallon up to?"

"I'm Dewey Draigle, the Chucker's nephew. They gave me five years for something I didn't do, that killing of The Braker. You'll remember that one. Even now I can't get away from it, so I end up here. Chances are they'll look for me sometime to take me back. It's like it's in the cards for me."

"You do as I say and I'll take a new look at things for you. Who's in there? Besides Fallon."

"Three hombres came along with Fallon and pulled me in from a card game one night, I suppose because I know the area. Names are Marks, Trevorne and Calimore, three toughies they think but ain't come upon you yet, Marshal. Calimore's awful fast and slick as a coyote. Watch him first. Trevorne's a simple one. Just muscle. Never killed anyone, like me. I think he's afraid to. Fallon's got him shaking. Marks is pure mean, born for beating things down, killing, but always needs the upper hand, like most bullies."

"What's Fallon planning?"

"He wants the next mail car on the Waco and NW coming in. Got a lot of money aboard for the bank. They're starting a new business, going to buy ranches, spread their wings. There's a lot of new business and it all means money … lots of money."

"That's scheduled for two days from now."

"They know that. The station master let it out of the bag at the saloon one night, at Momma Katie's. They got him slathered and he was choking up news of all kind."

"Here's what I'll do for you, Dewey. I'll give you back your rifle and you go to the back end of the cabin and sit by yourself. Help me if and when you can, but don't start anything any way but the right way. I have sent for a Ranger. Harry Cousins will be here in two days. He'll sniff you out quick as a wink if you mess up. Hear me?"

"Yes, sir. You going to really check back for me?"

"That's my promise, now get yourself back of the cabin, and as easy as you can make it, so they don't hear you. I'm counting on you."

"I'll deliver, Marshal, 'n' that's a promise." He thrust his rifle upwards, and Preshong felt the younger man's sudden enthusiasm and confidence. He had an ally he could count on.

"How long will it take, Marshal? Doing it now or later?"

"When are you supposed to get a break?"

"I'm here until dawn. Fallon said he'd pay us double what he promised, not that I ever believed him."

"We'll wait until someone comes out to stretch or wet, then we'll have one man less. You tell me who it is. I want to get that real gunslinger out of the way if I can."

"Calimore's tall 'n' skinny, Marshal, like a beanpole. I can spot him a mile away. 'n' he hates to wear a hat."

Preshong did not allow himself to get caught up in that trait, though it was an oddity in this part of the world; men used their sombreros as shelter from the sun, as barriers against the rain, as small vessels for watering their horses, for fixing the oddities of possession and subtle compromise, like cards, bullets, hearty breakfasts of eggs from nests found on the open plain, eggs whose shells would be crushed down onto coffee grounds dumped by hand count into their battered coffee pots. The range law said coffee grounds had to be stilled in the pot and life moved around the hats such men wore, so it was exceptionally odd that the gunslinger was out of line in that measure. Perhaps he was not a real cowboy. If not, what was he?

When hatless Calimore came out into the veiled morning, he was pinned against the twist of dawn as it lit about the cabin. And he was skinny, a tall pole for beans to be hung on, as Dewey Draigle had said. A thin presentation of a cowboy. He wore no hat! No Stetson, wide at the brim. No sombrero full of southern flavor. No tool for an ordinary cowboy.

Preshong counted him a loser. Saw him as a loser. Pointed his rifle at him from less than twenty yards. "Drop your weapons, friend, or you're dead. I won't say it twice."

For a moment silence hung in the air, and measurements of all kinds. Life hung in the balance of the charge. The words resonated in the early morning. They echoed . All could hear them.

Calimore, without a hat to mark him, went for his weapons. Preshong fired instantly, at the thin man's hands flashing for his guns, at the movement. The sound roared into the night, and brought the occupants out of the cabin in a rush.

Fallon the hero was behind two other men, stumbling, reaching for weapons, the three of them trying to see what targets they had. One man went down instantly, a round in his leg from Preshong's rifle, the entry mark blood red on his pants, his screams full of pain. Fallon and the third man, in a rapid calculation of where they were in the dispute, raised their hands in a quick motion.

Preshong saw it all develop down the road; Dewey cleared and exonerated of all charges; Fallon facing up to his planned crime, two others in his crew scrambling for the best they could find by spilling the beans on

Fallon, fast-gun Calimore placed in peaceful ground on the side of a hill just outside of town. Nobody else in the whole of Waco even knew what had been coming their way.

The cattle herds, though, kept coming for a few years, up the Chisholm Trail, across the Brazos River. More trains crawled into town from Missouri and Oklahoma, from Ohio and Illinois and Pennsylvania, and now and then a few freight cars never seen before, with the oddest names painted on their sides. The cotton on the small farms of the Brazos River Valley grew as good as any place in the country, the whole valley coming green and much of it leaving on the rails … cotton, corn and eventually the dwindling cattle herds leaving by the carload, and Butch Fallon, facing another eight years from a superstitious judge, was sent off without so much as a wave of a hand.

And Marshal Max Preshong, the star on his chest as shiny as ever, getting a bit longer in the tooth, marking his time until the end of time, walked a bit slower, a might cautious, now and then an image floating into his mind from some place locked in his past… or in his future. He was never sure from which direction the images came … as long as he saw them coming.

It was all a fair swap.

Covana from Wolf Hill

It was July of 1869, the day already beset by strange sights and signs, like human bones and animal bones found on the trail aside the hill flanking the wagon train, flesh long-gone to carrion seekers, long-bleached by the sun, and the howls of unseen wolves as if they were stalking each individual. The day had set the table for night, a sensation of anxiety crowding the travelers, alertness stark in all eyes, and all moves precipitated by widened studies of the area about them. These feelings ran through all the folks on the train as they headed west. Dark clouds, seemingly foredoomed, twisted out of other clouds before twilight. And distant thunder shook the ground beneath wagons as they circled at the foot of Wolf Hill. On the cliff-side rise to the top of the hill, odd and weird shadows moved as if coming to life, to spend time looking down on the wagon train, on the threatened campfires if rain came. The lead scout, shortly returned from his outride, said to the wagon master, "It's clear ahead for the move tomorrow. This place ain't never treated me none too good, this Wolf Hill, so have 'em ready for an early start. I'll be damned well outta here before your coffee's warm."

Even under these circumstances, beneath the gathering apprehension, new life had also made a statement. In the deep darkness a girl child was born in one of the wagons, saying life and death, fate and promise, and good and evil, were still at odds, still waged their everlasting war.

To find a name for their new daughter, who was born a flaming redhead, her parents drew letters from the only game they had brought with them from New England in the back of their wagon. The dull metallic container carried a plain brown logo and a legend that said, *Word Build*. Inside were small tiles with painted letters, four complete sets of the alphabet. The parents had used the word game often to help develop their language use in the new world they had come to, and decided to find the child's new name within the game. They drew, in turn, the letters *a, o, n, a, v, c,* and at her mother's insistence the child's name became Covana.

The game was never used again in this manner.

Some newborns, as we all know, come into this world unshorn, unheralded, and unwanted. On the other hand, some come into the most luxurious setting of all... into an abundance of love in spite of the hardships surrounding the birth. Wolf Hill, in the midst of a mountain valley of lush growth, presented both a rich and a harsh beginning for Covana Perkus, redhead.

Her father, Wulf Perkus, was from a dark part of Europe where legends and omens loomed continually in the minds of most young people and many of the adults. When as a boy he left his home in a mountain area with his parents, he carried all the area's legends and omens in his mind. None of them were forgotten and when the lead scout of the wagon train told them, "This place here where your baby got born is called Wolf Hill because the Indians long ago said a wolf stole up a child, so keep your eyes open for any slinkin' varmints." He pointed at the foreboding overhang of the escarpment. "Shadows live there. So we'll move on soon and get out of these here shadows."

The omens from the past, from the dark center of Europe, were still chasing Wulf Perkus. The name of the hill, the dark shadows high on the rocky face, the ominous look on the scout's face, told him about the chase. What else he remembered were the messages in some eyes he had seen in the old country, strange men in town, strange actions, stories following them, from school friends, neighbors, other story tellers who would nod their heads and cast knowing looks at the strange men.

But Perkus also recalled his grandfather's words from far in the past after a fear-filled night of storytelling beside a near-dead campfire: "Who fights the wolf and wins finds himself in heaven."

He could not shake any of those memories, the bad or the good, but a decision shook itself loose. "Marlen," he said to his wife, "we will build our house here. Our long journey is done. This will be our new home. We will fight the wolf and Covana will grow in a heavenly place." She saw more in his eyes than what she heard, and nodded agreement, but said, "This place will make you work harder than life meant you to, but I will too." She hugged her daughter as though she was a new-found amulet.

When Perkus told the wagon master and the scout they were leaving the train and would build at Wolf Hill, the scout shook his head and said, "Good luck, mister, and watch for them varmints."

Perkus was a prodigious worker, and their small cabin rose from the ground at the base of Wolf Hill. The garden spread its arms, a barn came the second year, and cows and a few steers the next year. It seemed as though they were in a detached part of the world, so little happened around them except growth of numerous kinds, and a small town coming into being a dozen miles away. Covana was in her fourth year and Wulf Perkus, as usual, carried a rifle everywhere he went, as if it was part of his arm. The wagon train scout had advised him that the sooner he got his hands on a Winchester Model 1866 Rifle, which many called Yellow Boy, he'd be better off. Perkus took the advice seriously and bought one from another wagon before it left. He proved to be an excellent shot with little practice because he did not want to waste ammunition and knew his day with the wolf, the day for the real entrance into heaven, was coming nearer, and he had to be ready.

This morning the sun struck at the shadows on the escarpment, and a few of them did fall away onto the bottom of the cliff. But some hung there as dark banners or streamers. Perkus took note and held the rifle closer as he stood on the small porch of the cabin, under an overhang he'd hung over the door. Covana was babbling inside and Marlen was answering her. Their voices were audible, and then they went away.

His coffee steamed in a mug as a chill hit him, not from the front, but from his backside. A cloud appeared from nowhere, the sun rays suddenly shadowed and thinned, and the silence in the valley became as clear as a breath of air. He waited for an animal to make a sound, like a cow waiting to be milked, or a steer or horse to make demands. Nothing further came from his daughter or wife.

He heard himself say, in a dark declaration, "I am in the eye of the storm."

That's when Wulf Perkus heard the howl of a wolf come from just behind the barn, and a quick wind coming from the same direction. The cow bawled as he ran around the barn and a black and gray wolf, of heavy proportion, had a grip on the cow's neck. Another wolf stood by the fence at attention. Perkus, without hesitation, shot the wolf by the fence, before he shot the wolf with the cow. A third wolf ran right past Perkus as if he wasn't there. His third shot dropped the wolf twenty yards after the round hit him from the backside. The cow shook her head and made noises in her throat. A big shouldered steer bumped against the fence as if in a butting contest, and Perkus knew he had to settle down his stock before he cleared the carcasses away and buried them outside the fence line.

His wife called from a shuttered window; "You catch that one, Wulf? Show him who's boss of Wolf Hill?"

"Showed and done, Marlen," he said, "Showed and done." For a minor celebration, he fired one round directly into the air, knowing it was a wasted round of ammunition, but it felt good. He believed his war with the wolves was over. And Covana, with the reddest hair ever seen on their side of the Mississippi, ran from the cabin into his arms.

"They'll know you coming, darling, even if they don't see you. That hair will light up the darkest places, including Wolf Hill. He promised her a visit to town as soon as they could get away, depending on a neighbor who would keep an eye on the place. It would take some time to arrange. He would never leave his home unattended, fearing the wolf would make a return. He never told Marlen that the wolf came in odd shapes, sometimes in different shapes, and always at a pretense. But he told Covana he would buy her candy goods. "They're as sweet as you, my flaming redhead." Where Marlen held her daughter to be an amulet, her father knew her flaming hair kept the wolf at bay much of the time.

As it happened, a young man from town waved at the family as he passed by a few times and finally came to their porch where he had coffee and biscuits and enjoyed Covana's happy spirits. His name was Tal Willoughby and he brought a broad smile and a noisy banter. Marlen enjoyed his good nature and his doting on her daughter. Perkus kept his feelings, as always, in strict reserve, but assented, after a few visits, that Willoughby was old enough to watch the small spread, and he would take Covana to town while Marlen, finding it difficult to leave her kitchen and not drawn to the clutter of people, would stay at home, at her stove.

Covana and her father were almost into town, when a sudden fear grabbed total control of the man. Parts of old stories leaped at him from dark horizons in the landscape. Once there had been a planned visit to the city in the old country when his father suddenly turned and started to run back toward their home, leaving young Wulf in his wake. The father kept yelling, "Hurry, Wulf, hurry. The demon is at home. He waited until we left the house. He is the terrible one. We must hurry. He is the wolf in sheep's clothing."

Young Wulf was terrified, fearing the real wolf, fearing for his mother, and out of breath from chasing his father. The whole scene was opened for him again. He felt the touch of air upon his face, the temperature, the crush working on his heart, the ache running free in his legs.

Now, as a father himself, the fear grabbing him about the safety of his wife and his home, he saw all the old monsters, all the crude shape of distorted animals and ghosts and goblins from the dark leap into his presence. The costumes reappeared, the disguises, the camouflage that desperate and evil creatures can evoke as part of their being. Did they hide in his barn? Had they always been there? Or in the root cellar when he was not looking? He set the horse and carriage at a gallop, with one hand on the reins and one hand holding onto Covana sitting beside him, her eyes caught up in amazement, her hair still red as fire, red as a glorious sunset.

"What, Poppa, what?" She held his hand tightly as the carriage bumped on the rutted road. "What is happening, Poppa?"

"The wolf has come," Perkus said to his daughter. "He has come to steal from us. Maybe he will try to steal the ranch."

"But I am not there, Poppa," she said. It's not the ranch. He wants to steal me. Momma said so, but I was never afraid."

"Why are you not afraid of the wolf?"

"He is afraid of my red hair."

"Who told you that?"

"The woman who comes in the night. The woman in the white dress who sits on the end of my bed and smiles at me. The woman who is not afraid of the wolf from Wolf Hill."

Perkus had no idea of what was happening around him. They came up a small rise, the house in view, the barn a dark form beside the house where the light in the window suddenly went out. He spurred the horse, afraid he was too late. The carriage tumbled and rumbled and bounced over the road. The howl of a wolf leaped at his ears. The cry shot past his ears as from a cannon.

"He is going now, Poppa," Covana said. "He is afraid of my red hair."

They stopped the carriage in a swirl of dust at the front of the house. Perkus screamed out his wife's name, "Marlen, Marlen, where are you?" There was no answer, but a dark figure broke from the front door and bustled toward the corner of the house.

Perkus saw the figure as the wolf. He fired his rifle directly at it, his eyes telling him he could not miss.

"Marlen," he yelled again.

The door of the root cellar opened. Marlen stepped up out of the root cellar. "It was that terrible boy," she said. "He is the real wolf of the hill."

Perkus made his wife and daughter stay where they were as he went to look for the wolf, or the terrible boy. He had no idea of what he would find.

At the back side of the barn, on the ground, dead as he ever would be, Tal Willoughby lay on the ground with a large red stain, already fully dried, spread across his chest. His young face was seriously darkened with a heavy growth of beard. He, without a single doubt, looked a thousand years old.

Wulf Perkus would bet that he was at least that old. In a way, the Indians knew he was.

Later, after a week of worry, talking to the sheriff and the marshal from the territorial office, seeking information about the young man, nobody in the town or on neighboring spreads had ever heard of Tal Willoughby. It was as if he never existed.

Wulf Perkus finally knew that the young, handsome, pleasant young man was no longer a man of mystery, for sure not anywhere near Wolf Hill. He would not say that about anyplace else on the way west.

Jacques Cree and the High Camp Stand-off

In the midst of deep thought in the fire-lit line cabin, solitude pleasantly surrounding him, ranch hand Pete Binchey heard the low, menacing, yet alerting growl of Jacques Cree come from the corner where his bed was. Slowly, in the shadows, as if not even disturbing the air or the meager illumination about his body, the wolf dog rose from rest, lowered his head, set his eyes on Binchey as though demanding attention, and stood immobile. In a quick series of images, the middle-aged cowboy saw the past history of the animal and the forebears that had nurtured the wolf dog's being. Nothing sounded in the cabin, and no sounds came from the narrow pass beyond them, where the Drago Mountain range had once been parted by huge glacier sleds of ice. But Jacques Cree was frozen in place. A bare breath of air moved from his throat, a paw rose in some kind of memory, some kind of message. Pete Binchey trusted every move the wolf dog had ever made.

The day had had such a good start.

Earlier, in the chill of morning, new ranch hand Pete Binchey left the small one-room cabin in the foothills of the Drago Mountains, his two horses heavy with chain and rope for hauling firewood, and the proud and faithful wolf dog, Jacques Cree, loping wide of the horses, forever keeping under cover. No training on Binchey's part had produced such behavior in the dog. Old survival genes and inherited shyness and slyness kept the animal among trees and boulders, bush and brush, shade and shadow, always on the prowl. Jacques Cree, six years old, part wolf and part herd dog, rescued as a pup from a rampaging bear, hadn't left Pete Binchey on his own in more than five years. Each one had paid the other with deep investment. To Pete Binchey, *dog-doo* had greater significance than the silly words frequently used by trail companions and saloon chums.

When the first snow fell before its due date, Binchey felt blind-sided. It was early September and the normal future suddenly had kicked him where it hurts. It had been a long while since he had been in the high country. Two days earlier the range boss told him, with some assurance, that snow was a good two weeks away and he'd have plenty of time to haul in additional wood to keep him comfortable until the pass froze over and rustlers couldn't use the pass as a breakaway route. As usual, Pete Binchey was aware of his responsibilities and his situation in the on-going world, the two notions often riding tandem with him, working on his consciousness; his weapons were in excellent shape, ammo was at hand, supplies closely guarded, eyes forever on the look-out, and Jacques Cree always his ace in the hole. At that moment Binchey could not see the gray face or the sleek gray body, or the deadly earnest, pale yellow-green eyes of the dog, but every once in a while a shadow would reveal itself with slight movement or a low growl would issue from a seriously dark patch of ground cover. The cowpoke often wished that trail hands had the same qualities as Jacques Cree, but, he'd snicker, that was expecting too much of any human being.

Now, early afternoon, snow coming a little thicker, a little heavier, the skies already dark as axle grease, his horses were straining to get the last of dropped logs back to camp. In one swing of the trail, the final log suddenly slid easier on the snow and the horses found it harder to get good footing. Eventually, with coaxing and a few harsh curses the animals had to understand, they arrived beside the small cabin. Smoke rose a thin, curling wisp into the afternoon air and the rich pine odor seemed to circle his head with welcome. Even the chilled toes in his boots accepted the greeting. With enough wood, he figured, he could hold out until he could scramble down the mountain, him and his two horses. And the wolf dog.

When the snowfall lightened considerably, and then stopped completely, Binchey spent the late afternoon hours working on the logs, sawing, splitting, stacking a decent pile by the cabin door and off the ground on slabs of rock. Jacques Cree, almost invisible, came to feed when Binchey put out a chunk of cow beef and bone.

Silence, after his tasks were done, seeped about the cabin like an invisible mist had settled over them. It seemed to come from higher in the range and also as if rising from the valley floor. In the awed silence, birds quiet, animal calls few and far between, Pete Binchey found an exultation sweeping through him; he had performed arduous but meaningful labor, the horses were rubbed and fed, his muscles felt sound and energetic, his disposition marking him as a happy man, the natural order of things advancing with his efforts.

He wondered how many men could enjoy the solitude that he found here in the foothills. On the wide prairie it was another kind of solitude that a man found, vaster, wider, but not as imperial. The domination of mountains would do that, he surmised, and then let the equation balance out. Of course, men in either situation would have to accept their place, or make changes. His own pass at sitting still, at an earned rest, allowed this revelation.

Jacques Cree breathed again. Binchey heard nothing. The paw came down; a half step had been made. The rifle was in the man's hand as the dog looked at him again, a half move to his head, the way a shadow moves in shade. For a moment the man marveled at the instincts the wolf had brought to this breed. Then he heard, over the cool earth, the distant neighs of two horses, one answering another. The live round was already jacked into the chamber; anyone friendly would have announced themselves a hundred yards earlier.

"Here, Jacques," he whispered. The dog brushed against Binchey's leg.

The first round came through the door, as if the intruder had figured the door would be opened directly, catching him in the act of opening the door or waiting for it to be opened with force. A horse snickered fairly close to the cabin. Binchey, settled in a corner, watching the one window, the rifle in his hands aimed at the door, guessed the horse to be thirty or so yards away. The bushwhacker would be in the small gathering of rock fall near the cliff face. It would be good cover against bullets but little against the weather. Night, with any kind of early vengeance, would make demands. He chanced a look out the one window and saw snow had started to fall again. Out there in the cold, whoever they were would soon get cold. He could count on that. He'd also count on any stalemate as one that would force them back to where they had come from, or rush him.

Realization said a bit of imagination often paid more dividends than bullets, of that he was sure. And all the tools were in his hands.

He whispered, "Jacques, the horses." With those words, and a sniff at a leather trace Binchey had used before, the wolf dog slipped out the door the way he was born to such movement, a shadow in shade, a piece of darkness in night, to do what he had done before for the man who fed him, wrestled with him, rubbed his head during the night, was ever his trail companion.

Binchey could imagine the situation with the bushwhackers; cold setting in, toes feeling it first or the fingers, bent in an uncomfortable crouch so as not to catch a bullet, their horses standing apart. If the intruders had donned ponchos or great coats, their mobility would be seriously hampered. All of it registered with the cowboy, the methods and reasons all predetermined.

The snow kept falling. Minutes passed as slow as the snow fell through the air. Another round, then another, hit the cabin. Binchey kept low, avoiding the door, realizing that impatience was at work, as well as the threat of a freezing night coming upon the shooters.

Another shot hit the door. A voice yelled out, "C'mon, pardner, get yourself out here or we burn you down. It sure ain't worth holding to this place. You gettin' a sawbuck for your time?" Then a second voice said, "He means all of that, pal. We ain't sittin' out here all night. You'll see that."

Pete Binchey could have counted, could have seen the whisper of gray slipping through the night, a thin coat of snow settling on the gray coat, as Jacques Cree moved in a circular fashion from the cabin to get near the bushwhackers' horses. If he had a watch, he could have picked the minute.

It was all simultaneous, the wolf howl almost on top of the pair of skittish horses, a cry that bounced off the cliff face and ran over the pair of horses like a terror let loose. The second cry was barely let out when the two horses bolted and ran right past the two men and went on downhill, the wolfish cry sounding behind them, bouncing off the rocks as clear as if from a megaphone.

A deep voice set a new tone. "Dammit, Harv, I told you to hobble 'em off to good size rocks. Now look at 'em. We got to quit this place now. Try to get 'em back. T'hell with this job." He started walking straight down the trail. "We got a couple tough hours ahead of us." Then, a bit farther off from the protective rocks, he added, "We're goin', mister, sorry for the inconvenience. We won't bother you no more. Was that your dog? Are you the hombre that once worked for the Bent Hook spread? Over Beaufort a ways? Don't have to answer, mister. Must be you. Give that hound a good hunk of beef tonight. He sure is worth it."

The silence came back, the pillow of it piling on. And the snow continued to fall as snow always falls on its own, without a wind, without a sound, being silence itself. Even in the darkness, the night swelled with it. And the wolf dog, back at wrestling, getting his head rubbed, leaned his weight against the man who kept on rubbing, who whispered his name over and over... Jacques Cree, old boy, Jacques Cree, Jacques Cree.

Fast-Draw Hickey

When the Quantrill Raiders left Bob's Village ablaze near Sherman, Texas in 1864, the only person left alive was a 14-year old boy who was working in a neighbor's well. He stayed in place, just above the water line, for almost four hours as the raiders killed all the inhabitants, young and old. He heard the voice of the leader (later declared as William Quantrill) giving orders to destroy everybody and everything. The smell of smoke and burning flesh descended to his hideaway during the four-hours.

The boy's name was Kinaid Hickey, first generation Irish-American, born in the spawn of a cluttered coastal city on the edge of the Atlantic, and rushed to points west by his father whose dream for full freedom was not yet completed.

When all was quiet above him, though the horrid smells still assailed him with a vengeance of their own, young Kinaid Hickey climbed from his place of safety. Guilt and condemnation carried through him when he saw the ruins of the small village. The cabin of his parents, their roof of sod like all the other cabins, was gone to ashes and smoke. Something told him he would never see his parents again; not alive, he admitted. Outside of the small breeze working from the west, silence reigned, along with the odor of burning flesh as it worked its way into his senses, every odor sharp as the sins of mankind.

That thought made him think of his father's Irish knife, a Scian Dubh, hot and honed on a grinding wheel. His father said his father had found the knife at the forge of North Gate Bridge, near the diggings around Christ Church Cathedral, in the very center of Cork.

"A knife from antiquity," he had called it, "our lone legacy from the past, along with our blood and our name. Preserve it as long as you can, Kinaid, with all the power you can muster."

Young but determined Kinaid Hickey stood rigid looking at the sights about him, sadness, loss, fear, anger, all working him into a dither.

He had to find his father's knife, now his knife.

But awareness came over him, a most compelling one that said, as if it had a tongue and a voice, an internal command with presence: "Quick, now, remember everything, every sound, every word, and every voice you heard this day. Remember names, even the names of horses that you heard riders call out. Remember everything, or write them down. From this moment, by all that pervades you, you are the sole avenger." Came then the realization: it was the voice of his father, as plain as the day that lifted itself off the prairie. "Avenge us," it said. "Avenge us."

In the distance, out on the span of good grass, young Hickey saw a

36

pair of horses feeding. One looked like his roan, Star, the way the sun rolled on his back, off his mane, dotted by his swishing tail. "For the chase, I'll have something to ride."

Later in the day, the smoke receding, the smells declining a bit, Star caught and tethered, Kinaid Hickey went looking for his parents. He found his parents' bodies, huddled in the ashes, what was left of them. Hickey, saying his taught prayers as far as they went, buried his parents beside the ruins, and then continued to search for the knife, his father's knife, the Scian Dubh, his legacy, his avenger. He found it stuck in a partly burned timber that was beside the ruins, one his father must have been working on.

The knife was whole in his hand.

He had his horse, a sidearm, a hat found on the grass, the Scian Dubh tucked in his belt, and set off in pursuit of the band of killers. At a trailside campfire, some travelers told him the Quantrill Raiders had been the ones scorching the area, looking for Union troops and Union sympathizers, weapons and ammunition for their own use, and killing anyone in their way.

He would practice fast-draws every day, for hours when he could, so he'd be as good as possible at it. Better yet, he'd be a magician with the fast-draw. He'd beat them all, including his parents' killer; he had named one man as the killer; he'd heard his name, Quantrill, heard his voice, and knew his horse's name was Greystock.

"Why do they kill innocent people who have not taken any side?" he had asked an old traveler met at a trailside campfire.

The old traveler, sore-wounded from the war, said, "If you ain't for them, you're against them, so you count nothing to them. Dead is as good as you can get for them."

"Are there Union troops around here?"

"Up the river," the old warrior said, as he pointed north. "Some up there, but I don't know how strong, or how long they'll be around. They ain't been doing so good, from what I hear. You going after them? They'll drag you into the ranks, same as Quantrill will do, but he'd as soon as kill you if you was to say no."

"I'll find the Union troops. I got settling to do." The look on Hickey's face told the old timer to cease his questions, which he did on the spot.

For a long year Kinaid Hickey sat on Quantrill's trail, through raids, firefights, disillusion in his ranks, plain outright mutiny, and now and then pure and unadulterated avoidance of stronger enemy forces. That trail took him out of Texas, into Kansas, Missouri, and finally into Kentucky. All the while, living off the land, on hand-outs and other small generosities of people like him, on the move, he studied the moves of Quantrill, before a raid when he could, or after the fact. He learned patience and planning and the difference between hatred and disgust. From a distance he always knew what murder was.

And he practiced his fast-draw every day, becoming so fast that he worried that he'd turn into a killer, the gun felt so good in his hand, so hot, so ready. He had become the magician he wanted to be.

During the long year of the chase, more than once he was forced to recede into the background as Union forces pushed continually at Quantrill positions or held their place in the war's schemes. He did not want to be caught up in the hysteria, or being suspected or convicted of being a Quantrill supporter. Nor did he want the conscription pledge tossed at him from Quantrill. Separation was important to him, and to his cause. He would not let anything intrude on his cause if he could help it.

That year also brought a sense of age on him, from the generosity of young women in high spirits, a few grandmothers who doted on the young and apparent homeless youth, and the sisters of rage who could never forget what pains had been inflicted on their families by or from different causes or reasons. The whole country had suffered, and much of it would continue to suffer at the hands of scoundrels, renegades, murderers, brigands, traitors, carpetbaggers and the raw cruelty observed from dawn to dusk that the war had loosed.

With such impacts, the revenge harbored in Kinaid Hickey never wavered in his journey, nor was it reduced by those he met on the way to its completion.

So it was, one evening in May of 1865, that Hickey was at the Three Borders Tavern in western Kentucky, after working for a month with his eyes on Quantrill's band secreted in one of three different hideouts he had discovered. He entered into a conversation at the bar with a Quantrill man he had identified weeks earlier and who had been sent to wait at the tavern for three recruits promised to enlist in the cause.

The Quantrill man said to Hickey, each having a mug of beer, "You ain't here looking for Bill, are you?"

"Don't believe I know any Bills around here," Hickey said, tipping his mug in salute to Bill, with his expression saying, "Whoever he is."

"Oh, if you knew Bill, you wouldn't forget him. A man for the cause." He is mug was tipped in salute to the unidentified cause.

"A noble cause?" Hickey said in a soft voice.

"As noble as they come."

Hickey leaned closer and said, as he tipped his mug again, "To Jeff and the boys," and swallowed his drink in one gulp.

"Amen," the Quantrill man said, and did the same. Then he added, "You wouldn't be interested in lining up with Bill, would you?"

"I will, sometime down the road," Hickey said, "soon as I get my parents buried properly. They were killed some miles apart last week and I'm waiting to get them together for all the proper ending. Least one can do for his parents."

"I like the way you talk, son, so have another beer on me and Bill. I'll be here next week before we move on, so I can talk to you again. I'm one of Bill's lieutenants," he said, seemingly as proud as a man could make it.

Hickey smiled, nodded, accepted the new drink and said, "Here's to a new page in our history."

"Amen," the Quantrill man said, as if he believed in grace, goodwill and God. "I'll catch up to you next time here." He left the Three Borders Tavern without having met any new recruits.

Riding back to his own hiding place, Hickey knew he had a week to set in place a few ideas he had been entertaining. The timing seemed perfect, the area feasible, and his intentions in place. At his backside, tucked into his belt, the Scian Dubh was as stiff as his backbone. In his open hand he could feel the mythic handle hard in place. A muscle or two twitched in his arm and ran up to his shoulder.

Sleep that night, after the long ride, was restless all the way through, but visions of vengeance kept surfacing as if wakeful dreams were enacting his coming days. They brought mild satisfaction in spite of the moments of glory he envisioned.

But, as many things happen to destroy or distort dreams, vengeance, and justice, the sweep of the war made another entry into the short life of Kinaid Hickey. A Union force had decided to camp in the area. From a hidden lean-to he had discovered in a deep thicket, Hickey heard the troops in constant movement of early morning, before the sun was out of bed. And still in the gray darkness of morning he also heard the rider galloping down the road below him yelling all the way into the campsite.

"Hey, Captain," the rider was yelling! "Hey, Captain! We found Quantrill! We found him! Sgt. Willoughby's still there, keeping him under observation. He ain't but a dozen miles from here and bivouacked like he ain't going to move for a long spell." He leapt off his horse and, with sudden realization, brought himself to attention and saluted his commanding officer rushing from his tent, snapping tunic buttons into place, slapping down his unruly hair.

The captain was not shaved or washed his face, but surprise gleamed on his countenance like a welcome entry. "How far, Corporal? How far did you say?"

"A dozen miles, sir. An easy ride, and he's got fast water on his backside."

"Lookouts, Corporal?"

"Like they was sleepwalking, sir. Like they never was trained to do anything the right way." He came again to attention, as if he realized again the situation and his appearance before the commanding officer. "It couldn't be no better, sir, according to Sgt. Willoughby, and he's regular army, sir."

Hickey had several immediate thoughts: he'd never get to avenge the death of his parents. Instead, the Union army would get to do the deed. And the second thought was his immediate need to get in with the Union force, to make his presence known, and then to carry out his original mission.

But he had to act quickly, and with conviction.

He washed his face and snapped his clothes as clean as he could so as not to look like a saddle tramp, saddled Star, and rode boldly into the campsite, announcing his way: "Friend coming in. Kinaid Hickey, last of Texas, with information on Quantrill's raiders. I know their campsite. I know their campsite."

"Halt in place!" a sentry yelled, and added, "Corporal of the Guard. Corporal of the Guard, a rider coming in with knowledge of Quantrill."

The Corporal of the Guard led Hickey to the unit commander. "Says he knows Quantrill's campsite, sir."

"Bring him in, Corporal," the captain said, "but keep your rifle on him."

With speed and quick-thinking, Hickey told the captain of his short life, the loss of his parents, and the sworn vengeance still working in him.

"I've scouted the place for almost a week, sir. I know they don't plan to move for at least a week. One of Quantrill's lieutenants was looking for recruits at the Three Borders Tavern, and let much of that information loose of his tongue. There's not a lot of camp discipline. They are a pretty loose bunch right now, enjoying some of the fruits of their thefts. Lots of liquor in camp from a recent raid, from what I can see."

"What do you want of this, Hickey?" the captain said.

"Just to be in on it, sir. I could be a scout for you. They've got water at their backside and I don't know why they camped there, except it's deep in a heavy glade of trees. It's as if they believe nobody can see them. If we get rid of a few sentries, we could walk in on them."

"You know the look-outs' locations?"

"Yes, sir. I can pinpoint them. They haven't changed in a few days."

"All right, son. You can go with us, but on your own. I take no responsibility for your safety, but I do want to get that man. Two of my men had relatives in Lawrence. You can sit in on our planning session. Add what you can. Go in with us, but in the rear after we take care of a few sentries."

40

Kinaid Hickey snapped off a quick salute that made the veteran captain smile.

They were not far from Taylorsville when they attacked the campsite of William Quantrill and his men. Shots were fired after two sentries were knifed in silence.

Kinaid Hickey did not get off a shot at the desired target, though he recognized Quantrill's horse and did kill that animal.

When Quantrill was taken off, severely wounded, to a hospital in Louisville, Kentucky, Hickey followed the entourage. A day later he introduced himself as an experienced orderly to the chief doctor who hired him.

That first night, after a full day's work, Hickey slipped into the room where Quantrill was sleeping, his wounds bothering him and keeping him wide awake.

Kinaid Hickey, now not yet 16 years old, shook Quantrill, held the Scian Dubh under Quantrill's throat, and said, "This one's for you if you get any better, which I doubt very much, but it's for my parents you killed in Bob's Village, Texas before you came this way. I have followed you every mile of the passage and I will not be denied my revenge until I have killed you fair and square."

It was early in the morning of June 6, 1865 when Hickey left the room, the infamous renegade still in agonizing pain.

Later that morning William Quantrill, killer extraordinary, Southern Hero and Northern Scourge, descending into his final sleep, died from wounds he had received near Taylorsville, Kentucky, a mask of fear across his face. Bob's Village, Texas, for the record, held no place in his mind. Nor was there any satisfaction or avenge in Kinaid Hickey, who headed west again on his horse Star, toward freedom and dreams, the Scian Dubh hidden under his shirt, stuck in his belt at his backside, the Irish legacy moving on.

As had been his habit for more than a year, he kept practicing the fast-draw, his hands slick as ever, perhaps faster than ever. Kinaid Hickey had become, for all the matter, a magician with the fast-draw and he believed it should not go to waste; he might become a sheriff or a marshal, he thought; there was always that need, heading west and getting there.

Gunsmoke Valley

The war had started. Not the Great War between the states, which was over by a few years, but a war in Gunsmoke Valley, a war sure to eclipse all actions up to that time. It was June of 1868, mid-day, the sun working like a stud, a horse limping into the Prescott spread, the Snake River in the distance like a slow rattler, poised.

Time, in all matters, in all elements, was exerting itself.

Luke Prescott's son, Thompson named but Tommy called, came home barely keeping himself in the saddle. Blood had soaked his shirt all down the left sleeve and against his chest where a huge blob of red shook Prescott right off the porch chair. The horse, still skittish from some kind of encounter, though well-trained at the ranch, had brought the lad home.

Prescott yelled to his wife, "Sarah, get some hot towels and water out here, quick." To his foreman Harlan Dobrie he yelled, "Harlan, take Smitty and go get Doc Swenson out here. Don't take no for an answer, if you can help it. Hear me?" He added, as he lifted his son off the saddle, "Tell Doc he don't come out here right now I'm coming to get him." His hand patted the pistol at his side; lately he'd be undressed without the gun belt in place.

Someone in the valley, Prescott swore, had put the Doc Swenson in his pocket. Just like the banker Holdsworth and young Jabber Cuscoe, running the saloon, had been locked away, declared. It had to be one of the ranchers getting bigger than what he was, and wanting more, fingers spreading into other holdings, other persuasions. He wondered how many people in the valley were touched, moved, like checkers on a board ... a flick of the fingers, a passage of coin. When he had time he'd think about who was losing and who was gaining in the valley, who might be looking to be bigger than all the others. None of them had been that way in the beginning. They had all been honest folk, bent to the task, making do for their families, scratching the better parts of earth to reach heaven.

And for all of that his only son may have been caught in some avoidable crossfire.

Prescott carried his son to the porch and laid him flat. His wife, with a pan of water and a bundle of cloths, began to clean up her son so they could check the wound.

"Tommy," she said, "can you hear me? What happened?"

"Who did it, Tommy?" his father said, the veins bulging on his neck, his arms shaking all the way to his fingertips. "Who did it, son? Who?" There was a rage touching on the air itself. Prescott sizzled in his body like a roast on a spit.

Sarah Prescott cleaned the wound. She had tended wounds years earlier, when the valley was first settled by wagon train folks, each staking a piece of land on either side of the river. She had experience and learned well. "It's a bullet wound in his shoulder, Luke. Looks ugly. Lost a lot of blood. But he'll be okay, I'm sure." Her hand touched the forehead of her son, easily, softly, but full of messages.

Prescott, somewhat subsided in his anger, still smoldering but marveling at his wife's demeanor, called one of the ranch hands and said, "Get the boys over here. I want to talk to everybody who's not out on fencing or line checking."

Tommy Prescott, bandaged, somewhat comfortable, his bleeding stopped, said, "I don't know who it was, Pa. He was in that thicket near the Twin Rocks on the river trail. I never saw him, but that's where the shot come from. I saw the muzzle flash right from the middle of the green, like the rifle was rested on a branch."

"You get knocked off your horse?"

"Yup, but he came back, old Charlie-T did, like a good horse. Nuzzled me like he knew what was going on."

"But you saw nothing except the flash? No horse rider earlier? Nobody coming up the river? Just the bushwhacker's muzzle fire? Nothing else?"

"That's it, Pa. But I was thinking while I was on the ground that this dude, whoever he is, could have killed me if he really wanted to."

He nodded and said, "He was that close, Pa, but he had to be setting there waiting on me or someone for some time. I didn't see any riders in any direction all morning. It was still out there, just a breeze in the grass. Not even a stray cow or a wild pony."

"All right," he said to a few of his hands gathering around, "get Tommy into the house. Put him in the front room. Then we'll have a little talk out here while we wait on Harlan and the doc to show up."

When seven of his ranch hands were gathered on the porch, Prescott said, "I haven't got the eyes I used to have, boys. Now you all know that. And I have to depend on you gents to do a lot of the looking for me, the kind I used to do back in the old days. That's part of your job, to keep your eyes open for the best interests of the ranch. It's where your money comes from, what some of you will use to get your own place going when the time comes."

One cowhand said, "What kind of things you talking about, Luke?"

"I don't know," Prescott said, 'but anything that looks odd or different or you haven't seen before. I've had a feeling for a while that something's going on."

All the time he was talking, Prescott watched Barnie Thrush, a hand who was a bit deeper than the others, who considered his options longer

43

when he had the chance, who acted quickly when he didn't have many choices. Prescott admired his stance on a number of issues. As he kept his eye on Thrush, he believed his ranch hand was into serious pondering.

"You mulling something over, Barnie? You look puzzled or unsettled about what I've said."

"Not that, Boss. Now and then, riding line or just being alone in the saddle, you get to thinking about things you've seen that don't have any good reason for being. I get that way. Like I got to have something to think about when I'm in the saddle and all there is is me and my horse and the grass under me and the sky over me."

"All this brings up something in your mind, Barnie? Something floating around without a good reason for being?"

Thrush, shifting in his place, knowing his thoughts were about to be exposed, and maybe for no reason at all, said, "I just wonder why Carlton Streeter's bought himself some dynamite when he don't have a rock or a tree on his spread that's in the way of anything. I seen him pick up two lots in town a couple of weeks apart."

Prescott thought that over for a while and said, "Maybe wants to dig a big hole and bury something, or just wants it on hand."

"Well, Boss, he's done it twice and both times he drove his wagon into town and that's all he picked up. Why drive a wagon just to pick up a small lot of dynamite. He could have rode his surrey into town or carried it on the rump of his horse. No need for a wagon."

"I guess I'd wonder about that, but he's probably got a good reason," Prescott said.

His attention was firmly grabbed when Thrush said, "And he covered the small lot both times with canvas. I was at the livery once and in the store the second time when I saw him cover them up. It just made me wonder."

Later, his son resting well, Doc Swenson checking him out and admiring Mrs. Prescott's nursing care, Prescott's mind floating things around, he said to Swenson, "Harlan tells me you were resisting a trip out here until he got real serious with you, Doc. You explain that?"

"Luke, you know I can't be everyplace at once. Two births are close at hand, old man Cloud's been a problem for a while, so I can't get too thin on my services if I can help it."

"Oh," Prescott said, "where'd you play cards Saturday night?"

"Well, I was at the D-Bar-D. Carlton invited me out." A nervous edge settled in his voice. "It was a nice evening. Priscilla made a nice meal for us. Why do you ask?"

Prescott said, "Cole Wrentham said he didn't know where you were when his foreman had that fall. No one knew. Jabber Cuscoe wasn't working at the saloon and on a Saturday night. Joel Didicker wasn't in the store, the banker wasn't around. Nobody knew where you were."

"Oh," Swenson muttered, "they were playing cards with us. Carlton invited us all out there. Priscilla had this great meal, like I was saying."

"Who won?" Prescott said, apparently cutting the conversation off, satisfied with Swenson's answer.

"Didicker won it all. Real lucky he was. Won the last pot in a free-for-all draw. Carlton dealt him an ace of spades and cursed us out of the house, in a nice kind of way."

"I'll bet," Prescott said to himself.

The next day, Tommy doing really well, his wife pleased, all hands at work, Prescott rode into Riverside to the general store.

"Hey, Joel," he said to the storekeeper, "how you doing. I haven't seen you in a more than a month."

"Luke, good to see you, too. What bring you into town? I heard Tommy got shot but he's doing okay. Glad to hear that." He was full of smiles and glad-hand stuff that bothered Prescott. "What can I do for you, Luke?" The good-natured phoniness was sickening. "Sarah need something special?"

"Not yet, Joel, but her birthday's coming. I have to blow some rocks apart on the other end of the ranch. I'm needing some good base stone for a new line camp."

"I can order some dynamite for you, Luke. Take a week or so. I don't have much call for it these days. Need half a case?"

"Oh, no rush on this, Joel. I got all summer to get it done, along with a few other things waiting on me. Don't want to get too lazy. Keep me in mind. A half case is fine." He waved goodbye and left the store, his mind still knocking things into place.

He knew he had cause for concern. He'd tell his hands to keep their eyes open. He'd even pick a few of them he really trusted to do long-search surveillances on the D-Bar-D. "All the little tid-bits added to the pie will come out in the cooking." His mother used to say that to him in the long ago.

More than a week later, his dynamite available for pick-up at the general store, the whole of Gunsmoke Valley as quiet as a mole, too quiet for him, he saw Barnie Thrush ride up to the bunkhouse and tied off his horse.

His saunter to the porch told Prescott that Thrush carried some news.

"You look kind of smug, Barnie. What'd you see that's got you this way?" He pushed a pitcher of lemonade to him.

Thrush carried a glint in his eyes. "You're right, Boss. Up there behind Crater Rock, but still on your side of the property, there's some

45

movement. I saw three drovers I know who work for D-Bar-D carry stuff in saddle bags. I'm willing to bet it's that dynamite they're squirreling in for later, 'cause they rode out after a short time. I couldn't see where they put it, but I figure they went into one of them caves up there."

"You're a good man, Barnie. You have a good sense of things about you. You'll do well when you get your own place. You and me, just the two of us, will be up there before light in the morning. We'll start out from the old line camp. I'll send you off on an errand later and you head up to the line camp. I'll meet you there. We'll keep this quiet. Don't tell the other boys. What they don't know yet won't hurt them." He looked into Thrush's eyes and said, "I don't want a real war to start and too many people get hurt. We'll try to do this without worrying too many people except those who were looking to steal something belonging to me."

He clapped Thrush on the back and said, "You got a stake in this, too, Barnie. I mean that."

"You're a fair man, Boss. That's all that counts with me. That covers everything."

He set off on his supposed errand into town, cross trails, headed up to the line shack.

Later, the sun long gone and night shadows for real in every corner, he heard the whistle signaling Prescott's arrival at the line shack. In darkness he opened the door, stood aside and heard Prescott say, "It's me, Barnie. Okay to light the lantern."

The glow sifted into the night and the two men slept on bunks against two walls. Night sounds they knew right to the species, settled the night with company, and they slept.

They had a quick fire, heated coffee, ate dipped biscuits, and mounted their horses for a ride, in near darkness, to the site of the activity.

After three cave searches, their two lamps showing things as they were, they found dynamite planted in several spots in the cave walls. They counted sixteen sticks, but not connected. In another cave they found igniters and fuse material. The two men carried all of it back to the prime cave.

In the flash of light, at one side of the cave, Thrush said, "Hey, Boss, look at this. This looks like gold to me." He showed Prescott what he had found.

"Sure does, Barnie. Let's check this whole place out before we do anything."

They penetrated the cave almost to the end where Prescott found the bones of a man who had been dead for so long a time they could not even guess.

Thrush said, "He's probably the gent who found the strike, Boss, and

46

never got to stake his claim." He looked at the back of the skull. "Here's what did him in. His whole skull in the back was crushed in. Could have been a partner who wanted it all, like someone we might know now, but left here to do the claiming, wherever it was, and the Indians got him or some critter did."

"You know what we'll do now, Barnie, don't you?" Prescott said. A ring of humor, subtle humor, rang in his voice.

"I got an idea, Boss, and if it isn't the one I'm thinking of, I'd like to twist your arm to do it."

"Okay, Barnie, you tell me what I'm thinking of."

Thrush smiled in the light of his lantern, a wide, incredible grin, and said, "Hitch 'em all up and blow hell out of the place. See what we end up with and who comes looking sooner or later."

"Right on, my friend. Let's do it."

They set to work and loaded, primed and connected every stick of dynamite they had found.

"How do we handle this, Boss?" Thrush said.

"We find what other cave's the best to hold off any troubles that come this way, like someone who might hear the blast. I'll stay here and you go get the boys. Half a dozen will do. It won't be a war if things break our way. How's that sound to you?"

"That's fine by me, Boss. You're probably sitting on a gold mine." He chuckled at that. "It was enough for this poor old gent to get knocked on the head, enough for people now trying to scrape it away from you on the sly."

The blast shook deeply into the heart of the mountain of rock. When dust and rock debris cleared the air, the site revealed a solid gold hit, a lusty vein angling down into the earth, throwing sparkles in the light of the lanterns that popped rich and often. They cheered each other, and Thrush ran to his mount and Prescott headed into the cave they had selected to hold off anybody with a mind to change ownership of the mine, or make off with as much of the take as possible.

A half day later Prescott heard horses approaching, men talking, and Carlton Streeter's voice saying, in a loud voice, "How do you know someone was blasting up here? Nobody could hear it if they were just a half mile away."

The next voice belonged to Holdsworth the banker. "I'm telling you, Carlton, an Indian told Craggy Harkness he heard it. He's got no reason to lie, not that Indian and not Craggy. If Prescott doesn't find it before we get what we can, maybe work the place for a few weeks, it'll be gravy for us. You convinced the others it was the only way to go. Prescott will lock it up solid and we'll be on the outside looking in at him rolling in what was an accident coming to him. You tossed that piece of rock right at his feet when you boys settled this place. You remember doing that?"

"Don't remind me of it again, Mr. Big Banker. You had a chance to have the whole hunk yourself too. So what did you do with it? Tossed it aside like it was nothing. Let's get what we can and get the hell out of here before Craggy or that Indian tells one of Prescott's boys. They'll light all over this place, like vultures on a dead cow."

Prescott put a round into the cliff face right over their heads, pieces of shale and lead bouncing around with a whiz and a roar.

Streeter and the banker and three other riders leaped off their horses and scattered in among the rocks.

Streeter yelled, "Who's up there? Why you shooting at us? We didn't do anything to you."

A second round, shattering rock with a ping and an echo, kept their heads down.

Their horses had run off on them.

"You gents rush that shooter right now." Streeter's voice was in an ordering mode.

"Rush who where, Streeter? Who's shooting at us? Why's he shooting? What the hell do we get out of it? This ain't your land. This ain't our job."

Holdsworth voice jumped in. "Do what he says. Do it now or he'll kill us all."

"Why will he kill us?" said another voice from further away.

"You damned fool, we're trying to get his gold into our hands."

"Oh," said the voice of Barnie Thrush, coming from his own hidden position further down the valley, "Mr. Prescott knows that all ready. That's why he's got these boys of his down here holding onto your horses for you gents. Just so you can ride back to jail instead of walking. He's mighty considerate that way."

"Who are you?" Holdsworth said.

"I'm just one of his new partners in this here mine we shook up this morning, nice and early. Ain't that right. Mr. Prescott."

Luke Prescott, holding his rifle like he was going to shoot it again, stepped out of a cave and said, "When we go into town, boys, and see the marshal, we're going to find out who and why someone shot my son Tommy from ambush. That's the next piece of business we do. The business in this place here is all done."

48

Hostage on Horseback

In a gift from providence or, the least of chance, from someone's carelessness, Cody Burrill had found a coiled lasso hanging on a small rock, as if it had all been planned, which he wouldn't believe in a hundred years. He found himself in a steep canyon as narrow as a rifle bore. As a cowboy, married to the plains and herds, rope and leather were his world, and now and then a shirt of denim, or, if his luck was better, some finery of lace once touched never letting go. Fabric held sway for cowboys, getting to town or just leaving town, no matter what the situation. And his situation was, or had been, as close to final as it might get. The coil of rope gave him hope.

He reflected on his past hours. Walking into the Bitter Creek freight office at the wrong time, after a pleasant night in the town, and finding a gun was jammed into his back. "Don't move, kid, 'cause you're comin' with us."

The voice said, loudly to the two employees standing with their hands in the air, fright alive in their faces, "We're takin' the kid here with us. If you start screamin' or shootin', we kill him right off."

The gun was jammed tighter into his backside and a bandana was placed over his eyes from behind.

"Move, kid, and don't mess up tomorrow for yourself." A shove came from behind, his foot guided into a stirrup, a push up followed and he was soon riding away from town in a rush. He thought he could count four horses in the pack of riders.

Cody Burrill was 17, still pink faced, though minor hair grew on his chin, being worn proudly. One moment he had been a happy looking young man with a joyous smile, the next second a young man full of anger. He did as he was told by the deep-voiced man, after weighing all things in his situation. "Revenge gets itself out of control," his father had often said, "though getting even is a joy perhaps not often reached but glorious when it is." There were moments such thoughts made him warm and fuzzy during that long ride away from Bitter Creek.

Hours later, he guessed, still blindfolded by the sweaty old bandana ripe as an old outhouse, the horsemen stopped. The ride had been a tough one, especially lately with many quick turns on rocky ground after long miles and a hard ride on good grass. In time he could hear mountain air as it whistled around tight corners, blew through narrow spaces, made music atop peaks of stone.

Within a whistling wind from above, the horses were drawn to a halt. "The whistling Margarita Range I heard about," he said to himself, figuring

49

out where he was ... the whistling peaks, the passage of time in the saddle, the sweat on the horse all making up his arithmetic.

"Off the horse, kid," the big one said. "You try lookin' after us, see where we go, one of us sure as hell'll put a round in your backside. They left him afoot in a maze of canyons, some blind and all tight as old leather dried in the sun. The bandana had not been removed once since it had been tied on his head. When silence came with a whistle of wind faint as a zephyr, the hoof beats fading to no echo at all, he pulled the bandana from his head.

Shadows flashed in his eyes, and a sense of darkness still existed for him despite the daylight. Sight returned slowly and he was aware of rock walls rising up around him, cliff faces looming as high as mere sunlight and making him feel as though he had been dropped into a prison cell. He was in a tightly constricted canyon, now sure he was in the Margarita Range. For all practical purposes, he was alone in the world, without a horse, without food, without a weapon. His future seemed tenacious at the very best. But he had hope. There always was hope with a rope, no matter what brand he put on it or what knot tied. In all the air he breathed, in all this Earth and the places he had been, the things he had done, this was, without a doubt, the pinnacle for him, for in this state of lacking all needy things, hope still carried his soul. It was a fuzzy feeling in his chest.

A normal coil of rope, usually saddle-borne, told him all that was so. Plain old rope, a coil of it, making statements for him. He half laughed aloud, but didn't, something setting in him, awareness taking hold.

And it was just then, at that moment of revelation, surely a sign from on high, that Burrill saw the body beside the trail, another cowboy lost forever. The before and after leaped into his mind, the birth and death and the short span in between came with a knock-out punch of reality.

It looked as if the man had been hit by a rock or caught in the mess of rocks that lay about him from some kind of rock slide, natural or arranged he could not tell. But something had happened to the dead man in an aperture of a canyon so tight that his escape would have been difficult. Burrill looked overhead for any tell-tale signs of further danger and saw nothing. The walls were steep but littered with cracks and crevices the way Mother Nature plays around with Mother Earth, roughing her up at times but always leaving her be. Continuation of things normal went through his mind.

Hope, with jumpy, jittery long legs, resumed its advance, crawled up his backside, lodged in his soul.

In a minor cave a little higher on the face of the cliff he climbed to get a better view of his predicament, to peek around a corner, he found a saddle tucked in behind some rocks. It was in good shape; it had not been chewed through by some critter of the night or a carrion feeder, no colony of insects taking over its leather world. A careful rider had taken care of it, as if he was posted here as a trail guard. If there were remains of a campfire, he had not seen them or smelled their leftovers.

He had the rope and the saddle but had little else, though. No horse. No gun. No food. For a few days he could get by without them, as water was available, slightly pooled in places from a fairly recent rain. He was glad he was not in the desert. To be dropped into the hammers of hell of the desert is one thing; to be dropped into the path of renegade Apaches, or hurrying Comanches, or drunken bandit he could envision further dangers. But hope had worked its way back into his thinking. Though he had a saddle without a horse, and a rope without a target, one might gain him the other. The fuzziness returned.

Thus, Cody Burrill was nearly lost in contemplating the new day coming on him as he came over the ridge, hauling the saddle and the rope, and wondering and what was coming at him. He clearly remembered what his father had often said, "Though it may have yesterday's brand all over it, today sure promises to be a new one, as it always is." The sound of his father's voice shook him out of his deep thinking, even as the old gent's voice said, "Thinking is for the campfire and the last part of the day. That's how you leave today's tracks on tomorrow. While you're high on that saddle, looking over what is around you, you have to be alert."

"What you doing up in there, son?" said a loud voice from a big man on a bigger black stallion with hellfire still in his eyes. The man, sitting the big horse with comfort and ease, had appeared as if from nowhere and was more querulous than curious, as the wondering fit his tone of voice. "You lost? You hungry or thirsty? You need a mount to get that saddle off 'n your back?" The humor seemed totally in control of his voice.

Cody Burrill, looking past the big man there in front of him, saw at the foot of the slope coming down off Margarita Range a crew of cowboys putting up a few hundred yards of wire, the poles already in place, breakfast still hanging on the air in a light draft coming at him. His mouth spoke before his stomach, the taste coming at him.

He didn't know what question to answer. "Yes, to all," he said, dropping the saddle and the rope on the ground beside him, sitting on the saddle, looking exhausted for so early in the day.

"Where'd you get that saddle, son?"

Cody Burrill, suddenly knowing what things looked like, said, "Back up there, in a tight little canyon. I think it must belong to a rider that was killed by a fall of rocks. The saddle was in a cave. It was put there or hidden, but there was no horse. The rope was around a rock."

"What kind of clothes on that cowboy?"

51

"A gray vest, kind of bloody now, and a blue shirt, just as bloody. Must have bled awful bad. Looked like he might have been kind of natty once he got to town, though."

"What did you do with him?"

"Covered him with boulders and stones so the critters won't get him. Wouldn't want myself to end up getting chewed all to hell and back."

The big man yelled to another rider. "Carlos, get an easy mount up here for our new friend. He buried Dixon up in the canyon. Looks like he got caught in a fall."

"Think he was trailing someone up in there?"

"That's what I'm thinking. I'm also thinking that some of our cows are up in there too. Tell Cookie to scrounge up some breakfast remains. Boy's hungry." He turned to Burrill and said, "What's your name, son?"

"Burrill, Cody Burrill."

"Well, Cody Burrill, I like the way you handle things. Like your code of honor for strangers. I am Stable Martin and I run the Bella Bella Ranch with my wife back there swinging on the porch but not as happy as she could be. We have need of another hand if you're obliging, now that Dixon left us."

The crew of men continued their work of fencing as Burrill finished his meal and Stable Martin sat down beside him on the back of a supply wagon.

"How'd you get up in there, without a horse?"

"I didn't do it on my own." Then he told him the whole story.

"You remember anything?"

"Yup, one or two times I got a real happy feeling when I thought about turning the trick back onto them, especially the gent with a deep voice. Sounded like Grant or Lee must have sounded out front of the troops."

"You in the army, son, or got attachments?"

"No and yes. I heard about it all from my father, who's gone now, killed in a bank robbery just putting in his few dollars a month for me. All that time at Gettysburg and other places, guys shot to hell around him all those years, and some bad-ass robber shoots him because he moved to step in front of a lady. Don't ever seem right, this world, and it's often that way, as he warned me, but there comes a time, he always said, and I could see the joy in his eyes about something done to him a long time ago and him catching up to whoever done it."

"You come over to the wagon son. I want to get that shirt off your back. I saw you a mile away in it. We ought to fix that. Anyone know you before will know you again, that shirt's so bright green. And we get another sombrero for you, or get that purple sage band off'n the one you're wearing."

"You sound like you got some suspicions, Mr. Martin." It was as much a question as a statement.

"You got a good head on those shoulders, son. You see things that ain't there yet, and hear things not said yet. I like that in a young man. My boy'd be just your age now, and like that, keen as a whistle. Was killed by a stampede by some rustlers we never caught up with. I know the fuzzy feelings you get, about making do on what was done wrong. I never did explain it to myself that way, but it says it all."

"Those suspicions of yours?" Now it was a question.

"Someone said once, beats me who, you can't see the trees because of the forest, or something like that."

"Meaning nearer than you'd think?" Burrill was trying to put things together, his brain working all the time. Martin had already opened up a whole passel of curiosity about "nearness." His suspicions were out in the open with a newcomer. The young man wondered who shared in those suspicions and who did not. The sheriff? His foreman? His hands? And why him? If Martin was seeing his son in him, or something like that, was he creating the same relationship, like Martin might be, on the other hand, standing in for his long-gone father? Had each of them made quick assumptions? He admitted to himself that his unusually bright green shirt and purple band on his hat were statements in their own, a young man's branding of sorts, a sticking out. This older man knew his ways.

Then Martin gave him some answers. "Lots of our cows get stole, but not many at a clip. It's why we're fencing this section, trying to slow things down. I knew you'd pick up on things soon as you opened your mouth. You hear things not said, see things not in sight. Not enough of that kind of business around here these days. Doesn't come with every saddle. Like I should have said a bit ago, my Maybelle is sure going to enjoy your company, Cody Burrill. She sure will, and it's about time for her to do so."

Cody Burrill sidled close to Stable Martin. "It'll be a pleasure to meet her, but I'm wondering if you have suspicions about your own people. There any truth in that? Like I'm wondering about changing this stick-out shirt for some dark, somber denim makes me look like a shadow, like low man on the totem." He crossed his arms over his chest like a teacher looking for an answer of sorts.

"I got to ask you, son," Stable Martin said, as if he was releasing any and all holds, "do you remember anything when you were blindfolded, other than the man having a deep voice. That could be anybody riding the range for a few days."

Burrill thought back to the freight office, the sudden gun sticking in his back, the bandana over his eyes, the ride away from Bitter Creek. He tried to compress details that rushed at him like a piece of a face from the past and him never being sure of the whole face, never saw it in his mind in one complete frame.

Details, he knew, mostly held their being in hard form; the shape of a knot in a rope, the tooling on a saddle, the color band on a hat that lasted for perhaps one cow drive or one sand storm, three white socks on a black horse, a rock in the trail you know has been trouble since it was left there by tumultuous Mother Nature a thousand years ago. Then the personal stuff came at him: a scar forever red and marking the face of a man as mean as the crime that produced the scar, the back of a man's hands that might tell a life story, the color of his shirt or vest like the wild green he had sported, when and why a man wore chaps out of the saddle, how pistols or revolvers were carried on a belt, the buckle on that belt, how a man looked at his cards in a game as if someone was looking over his shoulder all the time. Details were endless, and were difficult to call back unless something kicked them loose.

Going through all the options, he fished around for remnants of that experience at and coming away from the freight office, the sudden release in the canyon, the departure of the deep voiced rider and his two cohorts.

There it was! That little fact! Illumination! A boot in the stirrup of a saddle that leaped at him; the boot of the deep voice as it peeked up under the blindfold, the iron ring holding three straps and three rivets in each of the straps that crossed the instep, circled around from the backside, clutched at the sole of the boot. A leather boot man must have made them special for the man with the deep voice. Charged him a couple of months pay for those boots: brown, warm as wood, worth a couple of months riding the range, while keeping place and count for someone else.

"Yup," Burrill said in a sudden burst, "I remember his boots, like they was real special, got by a special order."

"Whose boots?" Martin said.

"The deep voice. He had boots must have cost him two-three months wages, boots I couldn't buy." He described them so carefully that Martin stopped nodding his head, as if saying we have him now. Instead he said, "My stupid ideas ain't always so stupid. Let's go see Maybelle and spread some cheer for a change."

In the course of one meal at the kitchen in the ranch house, in the course of history as one man might tell it, Maybelle Martin bloomed again right there in front of her husband, saw what her lost son might have become, found a dear heart In her chest she thought she'd lost forever. Cody Burrill could have moved into that heart and that house in a matter of one meal, but all knew it should take longer.

Eventually, over apple pie she said, "What's been going on, Stable?

54

You look like you've been into town and gotten the latest rumors. Am I going to be left out again?" Her hands were on her hips, but a smile was on her face.

"Well, Maybelle, the freight office was robbed, Cody here was there by accident, like at the wrong time, and they blindfolded him and took him along as insurance for their getaway, else they were going to kill him, like they threatened. They dumped him up in the canyons of The Margaritas and he found Dixon dead up in there and buried him under rocks. I think that's where some of our cows were being taken, into some place up in that mess of canyons. Got to be some place up in there none of us ever knew about. That's why we never did find any of our lost cows."

"Must be the same pokes robbed the freight office, wouldn't you say, Stable?"

"You're as smart as ever, Maybelle, and today a mite prettier. Don't you think so, Cody?"

They were laughing as a knock came at the door. Martin opened the door and a big man was standing there who said, "Boss, I think we got a few more cows that got run off somehow on the west pasture. Can't find head or tails of them."

Cody Burrill turned around at the table very slowly and looked at the man in the doorway.

Martin said, "Jake, I want you to meet my nephew hails from Texas and just up for a visit. Did you come across him at all on the trail? Said he rode in through the west pasture and saw nobody out that way. Whoever run off them cows must have already lit out with them. Know how many?"

"I'd guess a couple of dozen by the looks. Pleased to meet you." He held his hand out to Cody Burrill who had risen slowly out of his chair, and was still carrying a bit of laughter in his smile. "Me too," he said, and shook the hand offered by the big man.

Then Martin said to the big man first, "Jake, I want to show you something we found that may throw some light on this cow stealing business." He then said to Cody Burrill, still with a big smile on his face, "Cody, boy, would you do me a favor and go in my room over there and get those things on my bed. I'd like to see them just the way they were when I found them."

The young man from Texas, alert as ever, cleverly checking out details found in his mind, went into the room, and closed the door behind him. Chatter continued in the kitchen, and was going on when he stepped out of the room wearing the green shirt and the sombrero with the purple band on it. He was still smiling, feeling the fuzzy eternal goodness all the way down to his gut, and when Jake the inside thief went to go for his gun, he saw the rifle in Stable Martin's hands trained right on his chest.

55

Once trussed up, Jake coughed up everything about an inside gang that had been running off cattle and keeping them in a secret meadow way up in The Margaritas and taking them out another way. And let them know they had committed a few other deeds to get quick money, like robbing a bank here and there and a freight office when they heard money might be on the move. He gave names, each one of them men he had brought into the Martin bunkhouse under one pretense or the other, all ending up on the payroll, and all thieves.

The bunk house clean-out came in a hurry, right to the Bitter Creek jail, the guilty parties hog-tied and saddle-strapped the whole way.

In a matter of a few years the smiles were still on Maybelle Martin's face every morning, noon and night as she moved around her happy home, whole once more, gifted by a new son, and more and more every day Stable Martin sat with her on the porch during the long working hours of making a ranch move on into its destiny, in the hands of a promising son.

Grandma's City of Lost Names, Texas

They called him Chirp because he sounded like a bird with his high-pitched voice, but he was a mass of muscle with the softest hands this side of the great river. Because of its name, Grandma's City of Lost Names, in west Texas, nicknames were a pastime to which the citizens gave much of their time. There was a rush and a flourish to newborns, at first signs of naming, at first habits developed, such as with many of the Indian nations, and with visitors who gave any sign of a prolonged stay in the city limits and would harken to a new moniker of sorts. It had been that way, since Sophia Turfington Cornwell spent ten years in search of such a region, arrived at this illustrious place in 1833, loved every bit of it at first sight, claimed a piece of the grand land for her family, and then died on the spot.

Nicknaming was a game until it became notorious, with some first given names lost for eternity, such as the name originally given to the place by Sophia Cornwell. History begets history someone once said, but his name is also forgotten now. At least in Grandma's City of Lost Names, in west Texas.

Chirp was a second generation off-spring, born as Clelland Marshal Cornwell, and came to be called Chirp before his second birthday. His mother's nickname was Dizzy Lizzy, born Elizabeth Curtin Elsmore, who soon became EC El, then forced a name change when she danced onto that new name by whirling so fast and furious with Harrison Cornwell, known as Hurry Harry, one night at Rapid Tuckman's barn. She became light-headed, dizzy and fell in a heap at Hurry Harry's feet. Hurry Harry promptly proposed to her and she said yes.

The name stuck, as Hurry Harry never did hurry to get much else done in his life, but there was no going back for Dizzy Lizzy, she still loved him and the idea of a dance so furious people could never forget it. In turn, she often dreamed of going to Chicago or Saint Louis or New York, or even Paris, to dance on the stage. Sadly, that adventure was not to be; her name stuck in place and so did she.

There were side effects to such name calling, of course, mostly good and jovial in spirit, but now and then drew the devil on top of a person. And one could held back by the name itself, as if it belonged solely to him. Such was the case with one old man, Knees Jackson, bachelor, homely as a peccary, who spent too much time in his young years kneeling in front of any lady and asking for her hand in marriage. Needless to say ... so we won't.

Nickname calling also touched, without a sense of indignity or pity, the one-legged limping frame of poor Norman Leval Itiss, who simply and openly was called Arthur, sort of a left-handed nickname off the medical branch, who all folks prayed for when the word came from Europe that willow bark might be the miraculous cure Arthur needed for his own crippled knee. Yet Arthur was glad he didn't have Knees Jackson's knee malady, and looked forward to marriage and family in spite of his problem. Arthur, it must be told, got married, had children whose names escape us here, and became the chief teller at the bank in Grandma's City of Lost Names in west Texas, with enough land around for anything and everything imaginable.

So it was when a drummer, with a wagon laden with goods and sundry supplies such men carry, came into Grandma's City of Lost Names. For starters, we must be informed, his name was Carl Evert Tellerson, born in Boston not far from the seaport of Charlestown Harbor, where much of the trade of goods began at the wharves around the bay. Tellerson initially set up a tent to sell his goods, did well, and bought a store fronting the main street. He loved the packaging of goods almost as much as the goods, and it remains to be seen that some of his ideas have carried on to this day, of putting products into a package more valuable than the product itself. He had the ability to design or make or complement a product with color schemes, attractions that pleased the eye or the hand, and often masked some of his products with aromatic solutions. Smelly Telly became a fixture, began a freighter's company, then a stagecoach line, and bought the general store in town and in several other towns and settlements where growth came promised with each dawn. He was a rich man the day he died, and the weekly newspaper, *Nameless Tribune*, ran a headline that read, "Telly Wrapped Up."

But one of his sons bit off more than he could chew in the banking business, and ended up losing much of the family fortune. He was known as No-Teller Tellerson.

When the bank was robbed by By Jingo, who spoke a lingo nobody understood, he was shot dead on the boardwalk outside with a single shot by Sheriff Whowen, but usually called Where and sometimes Wherewhy by the real name waggers in town. By Jingo had come into Grandma's City of Lost Names in 1849, from the Baja Penninsula, and introduced himself as Dingle Ringo, and said he was a musician without an instrument. He sang a few ditties "in Mexico words," as he called them, earned a few drinks and made a few friends, cozied up to anyone who'd sport him a meal or an extra drink, volunteered to help in any community need saying in essence "the next time it comes up, such as a posse," and proceeded to rob the bank in late afternoon.

A new customer, coming in the door, yelled out in the saloon that someone robbed the bank.

"Who by?" said one customer.

"By him. By Jingo," was the reply.

"They catch him?"

"Yup."

"By Jingo by who?"

"By Wherewhy, Johnny on the Spot, with one shot."

"Someone write a song about that."

So, for all the matter and all the history of a place, which looms as a short time in the short history of Grandma's City of Lost Names, nothing boded well for that serene place the day the winds started to make announcements over the top of the mountains that seemed to circle this haven of havens.

The wind came up from the Gulf in a sprinter's dash, leaving its mark on much of Texas in the swath that the storm cut.

Harriet the Chariot

Harlot Charlotte

Gray Day in a Gray Town

It was a gray day in a gray town, somber, like the day after a holiday, hangovers plentiful, the sheriff still sleeping off a bad night and locked in one of his own cells and so far totally unaware of it, the stagecoach from Mercyville almost a full day late and carrying a delivery of canned peaches as a favor for Bart Hall of the general store, and the gruesome, merciless gunfighter Boxer Agrunts was newly arrived in Boothill Leveled, a new town barely 10 years old at the edge of the Snake River where it makes its sharpest turn in the long route south. The somber day sat atop him.

The sheriff, Kirby Nowell, was practically the first paper-pusher in town; most of his efforts, other than spending time in Sadie Kemp's saloon, The Ladies Kettle, was arranging wanted posters on the wall of his office, making sure on every prudent occasion to hide a poster if the subject came into town. His next big arrest would be his first and he had not heard that Agrunts was visiting. Nobody in Boothill Leveled had bothered to yell the news in through the open door of the sheriff's office and two-cell jail; why wake him up just to cover Agrunts' poster on the board with a poster of Jack Gruden, long dead, or Wiley Lockburn, already six years in solitary in Yuma Territorial Prison, or Smooth Billy Two-guns, now probably 91 years old and known to be living in New York City on a bet that he must have won by this time?

The best business man, most lucid and cogent individual in town, the true pillar of the community, was the owner of the store. Bart Hall had built the store, the first structure when the community started, because he could see the river just below making a grand turn in the geography of its long run, and knew what it would eventually bring to any place on the site, where the dead from an older settlement had been buried without name, memorial, or precise location, except as said "on that grumpy little hill over there where the dead guys are buried." So Hall called the place Boothill Leveled and the name stuck just as did the name of his store, Boothill Leveled Trader, which people simply called BLT, and which now was out of canned peaches.

Canned peaches, for the outlander to the western plains, without the simple knowledge of trail drives and inherent needs of drovers coming into a town, dust in their lungs and throats, mouths dry and sweetness unknown for weeks or months at a time, unless they had dared open a bee's nest. Other than beer, whiskey or a friendly face, there was nothing like a can of peaches to have as one's own, or, for the best of friends, to be shared apart from all other hungry folk, outside town, or at a campfire, or behind the livery before the horses were taken care of, like good cowboys did.

Agrunts voice was rising in its declarations. "Whadyamean, you don't have no canned peaches?" He had come into the store smiling, the calling in his throat, that sweet taste, that overcoming pleasure, solace coming so close to the deprived.

"Of course you have some canned peaches. All stores carry canned peaches. I seen them in every store in every state and territory. Peaches. I want my peaches."

Agrunts' eyes were alive, lit up like a cindered orb, like the orange-red moon of October nights. "That's all I want, a can or two of peaches. You probably got them hidden under the counter or in the back or in some secret overhead hiding place, put away for your favorite customers, like the saloon owner or the damned barber or the sheriff or the mayor or whoever runs this place these days. Favored customers, not someone like me, get the peaches."

His body swayed in place, seeking balance and equilibrium, determining proper posture, his hands suddenly as itchy and dry as his throat. "Well, it ain't right and I aim to get my peaches," and with that he went for his gun to aim it at Hall behind the counter, who was a might quicker for a common dispenser of canned peaches and had a double-barreled shotgun on his hip like he had been shooting squirrels in the trees at that precise time and knocking out their eyes at fifty feet.

There was not a single token of shaking in Hall's hands, the shotgun steady, its aim clearly mid-section of Agrunts' wide and flabby frame with his hand hung in the air as if he was measuring death or peaches sliding their smoothness and sweet texture upon his tongue before he'd chaw a peach half into quarters, finding salvation from the trail.

Agrunt started shaking, convulsing, his eyes playing tag with each other, hiding, coming back from the top of his head, the whites of them on parade.

Hall held the shotgun steady. This man in front of him was a terror at murder and holding up banks and robbing the new trains running across the wide grass of the plains to little towns like Boothill Leveled, generally supplying BLT with all its needs. He had read the poster on Agrunts, felt like he knew the man. Now the stage was late with his special order. He'd paid extra for it. No free shipping out here in the west. No one-day specials for him.

He felt he was at a stand-off. He didn't want to shoot a man over a can or two of peaches, but the man was shaking, the robber was shaking, the notorious bandit and killer was shaking. Hall had to protect himself if it went any further. His finger tightened on the trigger; he got himself ready for a No Sale

Agrunts, still shaking and convulsing, nerves perhaps gone to pot, in

61

a mood of moods that controlled his body, set his mind, began to cry like a baby. He sat down on the floor and kicked his boot heels on the floor, and pounded out his sadness and loss, and suddenly began to cry. His pistol fell noisily from his holster and skittered on the floor. He did not even look at it.

"I want my peaches," he said. "I want my peaches." He sobbed it out, "I want my peaches," his voice falling away into unintelligible words, and came back to plead, "One simple can of peaches."

Hall subsequently, a tear in his own eye, escorted Agrunts, with the bore of the shotgun at the wanted man's back, to the jail.

As inevitably foreseen, the sheriff was still sleeping off his hangover, and still in a locked cell. The other cell was empty. Hall searched the desk and the wall and could not find the key to the other cell. He was about to give the whole thing up, let the prisoner go, apologize for being out of peaches, when Agrunts screamed the most joyous of screams, and raced to one corner of the office, and picked off a single shelf holding a shaving mug and a razor and a bar of soap, one #10 can of peach halves.

And Agrunt began crying again as Hall, retrieving a crude opener from the office desk, began to open the supposedly only available can of peaches in Boothill Leveled, on the banks of the Snake River, and the stage still late with the special delivery, the single available can clearly bearing the embolden identification of "Ogden Canning Co., Utah/Peaches."

Agrunt, sitting at the sheriff's desk, his mouth watering as he prepared to sink his knife into a delectable peach half sitting at the top of the opened can, did not even notice his poster prominently displayed on the sheriff's poster board.

His gray day had gotten brighter.

Dog Bone for the Bounty Hunter

His father's past had holes in it, questions, great open areas, but his mother had always said, "Shush now. Shush. He'll be back soon's the job's done he went to do. It may be a while. We'll keep busy doin' what needs be done." She had soft eyes and leathery skin that the sun no longer bothered.

With her hand shielding her eyes, she followed the slimmest shadow of her husband, Burt Steggins, going over the last rise out on the grass. Every time he went off she made the same moves, loved the shadow she saw, knowing it was part of her man.

"What's he doin' all the time, Ma? You never told me once what he does, never mind me askin' him who don't talk much."

Young Herald Steggins was 12 years old, big for his age, good with plow, rope, a team of mules, any horse and any weapon, and a big dog he called Hardtack that he could almost make dance. He was crowding 13 like it was tomorrow, when he too saw the shadow of a man disappear out on the grass, like it wasn't there in the first place. He remembered always wondering about the man who was his father. Beside him was his dog, black as night and big as a wolf. The dog never seemed to leave the boy's side.

His mother said, "Thems that need him call him for the work. When he's done there, doin' for them, he comes home to us."

"Allus bringin' a present for you, Ma, and somethin' special for me, like we was waitin' all the time for it."

"Yore pa's a good man, Harry. Someday he'll speak a whole lot about what he does a whole lot." Her hand, hard with ranch life leaving marks on it, touched his shoulder light as a shadow.

Five weeks later, Burt Steggins had not come home. His wife Martha sat out front of the cabin every evening as the sun set down on the home range, the mountains looking like fire was on them and her trying to see a dot of a man coming across the grass with the red sun behind him.

Harry pestered her no end, saying, "I ought to go lookin' for him, Ma. It falls on me. You can't go. I can't leave you, less someone's here spendin' time with you, helpin', gittin' by til I come back with Pa. So what'll we do?" One hand dropped onto Hardtack's scruff and lingered there. The dog wouldn't move with Harry's hand on him, moved only at trained commands sent by that same hand or by Harry's voice.

"I've sent word to cousin Lovell Dunkirk, sayin' we need help. He'll be here soon's he knows, then you can go."

"You sure, Ma? I hope so. I can't stand no more o' this."

"You go lookin', Harry. Your pa all this time's been a bounty hunter.

They sent word they wanted him in Foster City, to track a gent raisin' some special kinda hell out there. Sheriff knows Pa from way back in Sugarland. Name's Luther Stemwick. Go see him when cousin Lovell shows here. Luther Stemwick, sheriff, Foster City."

A week later, after the arrival of Lovell Dunkirk, Dunkirk smooth in the saddle and with his talk as any man ever met, better looking than the barber in town, young Steggins rode out the same way as his father had, casting a shadow the grass swallowed all too soon. Hardtack was right behind him, all the time looking back the way they had come.

In Foster City, in Luther Stemwick's office built against the side of the Foster City Bank & Loan, Harry Steggins said to the man sitting behind a small table he thought was supposed to be a desk, "Sheriff, my name's Harry Steggins and I'm lookin' for my father, Bert Steggins, you asked help from, a bounty man who ain't been home in 6 weeks or so."

"I been wonderin' about him too, son, since he left here more'n a month ago."

"Who's he chasin' down? Who'd you send him after you couldn't chase yourself?"

"Yore pretty crispy, ain't you son?" the sheriff said. A tired face sat under his Stetson, one bullet hole near the crown as plain as a wart, him moving around in his chair with a sure itch working him over. When one of his hands started to shake a little as it sat on the table, the sheriff moved that shaking hand into his lap.

Finally, with a sigh limping from him soft as a curse, Stemwick stood at the table serving as his desk, lazy looking to Steggins, too round at the belt like he couldn't go too far on his own two feet if his life depended on it. And he was wearing a sneaky look, the same kind Steggins had seen on Lovell Dunkirk's face, as if they had all kinds of things planned to make themselves better.

"My ma sent me to look for my pa. You don't tell me nothin', I go lookin' on my own. I don't owe anythin' to anybody 'cept my Pa and Ma."

"Man's name is Hurry George. That's all I know. Big, hulky, like a Clydesdale on a freight line. Kilt three men, one woman, a kid no more'n 10 years old, like in a few minutes of shooting not much more'n a month ago. Swore forever he'd never go to jail. Lives, far as we know, up in the Rockies deep as a man kin go. He's kilt two deputies went lookin' for him, far as I know. Maybe more. He's wanted by every lawman from here to Independence City."

"Why'd you ask my pa?" Steggins, not bashful at all, stared into the sheriff's eyes with the direct stare only the innocent can muster.

Stemwick nodded, shrugged one shoulder, and said, "Boy, your pa's better than any my deputies. The fact is I can't spare any more. Hurry

64

George kilt two of them and I'll run out of 'em and be alone. Can't do that." He measured an added fact, then said, "I sent him, yore pa, out lookin' for the Testa brothers one time an' he brought 'em both back, and hell, if he don't git a hold of Luke Carbornet on the way back and bring him in too. Must've celebrated with yore ma over that. Brought some wine home, a new dress, I'll bet."

Steggins saw a sorry look go across the sheriff's face, the way he saw a cowboy look at another cowboy once who was getting up on an unbroken stallion with a burr under his blanket, put there for real teasing.

"I'll go lookin' for him. See what he says about my pa." He turned toward the door, turned back and said, "When I find what's happening, see Hurry George, I might come lookin' see if you need a real good deputy."

"How old are you, boy?"

"Old enough to git kilt, sheriff."

The sheriff thought the boy was finished talking, but he turned and looked back at him, straight in the eyes again, and said, "On'y if'n my dog lets him whoevah."

"Well, son," the sheriff said, "you go up in there, make sure anythin' give you a sign, move yourself behind somethin', 'cause he shoots from shadows, darkness, hidden places you don't suspect. A rat shooter, he is. A bushwhacker all the way. Man was born mad and gets madder all the time." Then he said, having moved to a window, "Is that your dog out there, the black one? He come with you, tag along all the time? He trained like you say?"

"Can do tricks, what I tell him, knows how to round up horses, scare cattle, chase the mules all the way home. Can almost git his own supper."

Harry Steggins, now 13, smiling at the sheriff, having an upper hand, rode out of town, his dog at his heels looking behind them every few minutes, scaring some of the people on the street going right through the center of town.

For four days Harry Steggins tied his horse off in hidden areas and went searching on foot through the mid-range of the mountains, his eye always looking for signs of Hurry George. Hardtack was a silent, stealthy companion, crawling when his master gave the word, standing still another time for 10 or 12 minutes, his nose in the air. On the fourth day Steggins, alerted by Hardtack, smelled something cooking, followed the smell coming out of a gorge entrance he had passed a couple of times. A shift of wind brought the odor of cooked meat down through the gorge and right into his nostrils. Hardtack's tail twitched lightly.

"Supper's on, boy," he said, "but they's plenty for tomorrow." Then they faded into a rocky background.

The next two days, from higher up in the rocky tor, with a spyglass his father gave him after one trip, he watched Hurry George as he plied his way between a cave and a fire pit outside the cave. A couple of times, when Steggins really thought about what he was looking at, he realized the man was bringing food into the cave … after he had eaten his own share.

A surprising hope started to build in him that his father was a prisoner in the cave, or somebody else.

The whole scene had to be set up in his mind, right down to each detail. And most important to him was getting between Hurry George and whoever was in the cave, hoping it would be his father.

Steggins spent that night, back with his horse in a hidden area, no fire, chewing on hard biscuits and jerky, drinking water from his canteen, keeping Hardtack watered as well his horse, thinking about his father's homecomings. The sheriff's words came back as he remembered one return when his father came with a bottle of wine and a new hat for his mother who said she'd save it for next year. But he also brought three new dishes and a couple of sharp knives for her. He couldn't remember what his father had brought him on that return from bounty hunting. It didn't seem very important now, unless it was the spyglass. He touched it with his fingers.

In early light, with Hardtack hidden behind a rock, Steggins studied again the movements of Hurry George, who led his horse to a small spring of water seeping out of a mountain crack. Then the killer carried two canteens full of water back into the cave after hobbling the horse. He spent no more than 10 or 12 minutes in the cave. The fire, kept as far away as possible from the cave to prevent quick discovery, was fed from a pile of wood stashed in under one ledge. The pile was nearly depleted and Hurry George, as he had a few days earlier, would leave the gorge and come back in less than an hour with a bundle of wood tied in a blanket on the rump of his horse and another bundle in his arm.

Young Steggins and Hardtack sat still for two hours until Hurry George grabbed his blanket for toting wood and mounted his horse. On his horse, he yelled into the cave and waited. A near mute reply came out of the cave. Then he rode down the gorge and went out of sight. Steggins and Hardtack slipped down off the higher ledge and entered the cave.

It was dark. Young Steggins was right behind Hardtack who had only gone a few yards and the dog almost hummed a growl.

"Pa, you here?" he said. Hardtack let out a soft yelp.

"Be still, Harry. No talkin' but cut me loose quick. My hands and feet are tied real tight. You got your rifle?"

"Yes, Pa."

"Hurry, boy. Git that knife out. There's a girl in there deeper. We'll cut her loose later. I owe this critter."

His voice was hard as beat tin. "I don't care if you break skin, Harry, but cut these ropes. Do it quick. He don't take long to git wood. Just picks it up, what he can handle. Hurry."

The knife was quick. Hardtack paying attention to the deeper part of the cave, the darker part, a continual sound in his throat.

"He won't come real close less'n I answer the right way. You gotta be out of here and away when he gits back. Might have dynamite here. He's awful tricky. When he calls, don't let him shoot into the cave. Don't give him a clear shot. I swear he's got somethin' gonna break loose somehow or other."

He thought for a second. "Put some little thing out of place out there, draw his eye, make him slow down."

Standing, one hug for his son, he said, "Take yore rifle, give me your pistol. Make the shot count. Git him in the left shoulder. Hurry."

"Git now," his father said, and Harry Steggins ran with Hardtack at his heels. He looked around outside and set Hardtack up on a ledge nearer the entrance to the gorge, patting him down in a prone position, whispering to him, touching him again. Then he climbed back out of sight, but over the cave, not away from it. He wanted to place himself between Hurry George and his father … and the girl he had not seen, deeper in the cave. He remembered what his father said about grabbing the killer's attention and threw a bone Hardtack had been chewing on out onto the rocky floor of the gorge. It hit with a cracking sound.

Less than 15 minutes later Hurry George, loaded down with scrub wood in his arms, rode back into the gorge. He stopped in place, cocked his head, listened, put his nose in the air as if a new aroma had been discovered. Two or three times he looked around, as if trying to see what had changed. He was half conscious of the chewed bone on the rocky floor.

Hurry George's voice rang out in the gorge. "Burt, you wantta eat?" He still sat his horse, still had his head cocked to one side, trying to settle something in his mind.

"Same as ever, Hurry, stuff it. I don't eat no more off'n no animal what tortures a girl, beats a man who's tied up 'n' can't fight back."

That's when Harry Steggins, hearing those words, anger and frustration coming like a flood over him, stood up, aimed his rifle and whistled. Off the cliff ledge came the black cloud of Hardtack fully airborne, a growl coming from his throat deep as a canyon sound, but more frightening.

Hurry George's horse reared on his hind legs, tossing rider and armful of wood and blanket full of wood to the ground in a wild scramble.

Leaping up from the ground, his horse struggling to gain control of four legs, Hurry George saw the youngster on the ledge, heard a growl from behind him, heard his horse's hoofs striking the rocky floor of the gorge, and tried to draw a side arm. A bullet slammed into his left shoulder. When he fell to the ground, his pistol loose, the open jaws of a black dog were almost at his throat.

Hurry George screamed. The black dog did not move. The shooter on the ledge stood still, a smoking rifle in his hands, and Burt Steggins, bounty hunter, stood over Hurry George with a pistol aimed right between his eyes.

The pair of Stegginses had him hog-tied in a hurry, stuck a clean cloth against the wound, and promised him a doctor, "If we git time to do it."

"Harry," said his father, "watch him. If he moves shoot him in his other shoulder, close up. Make it hurt. I gotta check the girl. She been cryin' for a week near. Think she goes hungry."

He went into the cave, stayed less than five minutes and came out with a girl with dark hair, pale skin, bruises on her face and arms, but a light in her eyes. Sobbing, she hugged the elder Steggins as he carried her from darkness. Her dress was in tatters but she didn't seem to notice it.

"This here's Alma Coombs, Harry. This crazy feller kilt her folks, all o' them. She's comin' home with us, after we take him to the sheriff in Foster City, tell her story, git us a payday, git this gent hung proper, sure as breathin' free ag'in."

He put Hurry George over the saddle of his horse and tied him underneath, a rope cinching hands to feet. Alma Coombs he sat on the saddle of Harry's horse, sitting tight against the son, her arms around him. She was a fourteen-year-old girl who was now a woman.

With Harry's rifle in hand, Burt Steggins led the two horses out of the gorge, setting off on a slow walk back to Foster City.

He was wondering how his wife was, when Harry said, "Pa, what you bringin' Mom this time, 'sides a new daughter?"

Gregory Tolliver, Tascosa Gunsmith

In his heart and mind, down in the core of his nerves, Tolliver knew momentum had started anew in Tascosa.

The newest stranger in a black hat and a vest matching its color and trim was riding into Tascosa on a magnificent black with one white sock. Only Tolliver the gunsmith took note of everything as he sat in front of his shop, the evening sun sloping on him and the rider, shadows getting long legs. It was said of Tolliver, settled in Tascosa for almost ten years, like a native son, that he had the eyes of a Pawnee scout and the fingers of a piano man. Those eyes measured the stranger on the big black, as his fingers twirled on the makings of his own smoke. Tolliver was unhurried and content, but he was intent. Behind his shop counter he'd be intent, as he would be on horseback or sitting there in the sun, his character always in place.

Behind him the display in his shop window showed a collection of hand guns and rifles worth a lot of money ... each prime weapon and a scattering of shot guns on display. Tolliver's reputation was founded on a number of things ... contest winners who used weapons beyond belief, lawmen who moved with longevity, sharpshooters who could excite a town into instant attention by way of a bank hold-up or a sheriff shot dead in the main street, or a quiet game of poker in a corner table of a quiet saloon suddenly gone amok.

All of those characters needed and wanted guns with the quality of Tolliver's guns. He didn't make them, but he brought them to perfection with his good eye and delicate hands.

The first note Tolliver mentally locked away about the stranger centered on the pair of guns sitting in dark holsters riding on his hips, in rhythm with the bay's hoof beats, as if they advertised the music of a shooter. To Tolliver, the man without doubt was a shooter, an out-and-out shooter. He marked him a snap-draw artist, quick as a skittish colt, sudden as a puma's leap, the kind of a man who walked away from duel s in the one dusty road running through too many towns. In spite of stories always circulating about him when shoot-outs and duels were discussed, Tolliver found a certain liking for the man. He supposed it was his bearing, the aloofness, the confidence sitting around him, like a protective wall. That clued Tolliver back to his own younger and exciting days. And he knew this man's name; Teal Forsythe.

The other man was already in town. He had come earlier in the week; Judah Pawkins.

In his ten years abiding in Tascosa, he had never misjudged a stranger's roll in life. And often knew what had brought a new man into town … some man, like this new stranger, Forsythe, high on a horse, well-dressed, cool as a morning breeze, was already there, as if the telegraph had aired a boxing match … the contestants are now available. All, he thought, in line with his own sole interests of making a living, which was the propulsion of solid lead pellets through the air with unerring accuracy.

Tolliver, hands down in all of Tascosa County and in the whole territory, long reigned as the best at his craft. Dead men, a lot of them in their own negative way, spread the word … Tolliver's guns gave any man the edge in a draw down, the duel at sunset, pushing the pellet where it was meant to go, its direction so accurate there was little room for replay, or little time.

As he studied Forsythe upright in the saddle, a polished shine broke loose from his gun handles when sun rays struck them, the way subtle arguments or advertisements are set off. Cheap publicity for the price. The handles, he was thinking, were smooth as plow handles or old reins touched with the sweat of a man's hands. Response was built into the smoothness, how they'd slip from leather pouch to a pair of hands quick as a jack rabbit at escape. Tolliver, at another speed, in a rare return to a prior form, felt the old stance, the hand movements, the acceptance of destiny, life often in the balance … there'd be a move, a shot, a man would fall. It had never been him that did the falling.

Forsythe, at another quick study, looked tall and lean, and the gunsmith saw how the stirrups were set at a low point, for comfortable riding or easy mounting. He'd wait to make up his mind on that point, his thinking finding itself centered on another man, the other stranger who had come into town a few days earlier, the one and only Judah Pawkins, gunsmith in his own right, but from the other end of gun work.

Many roads led to Tascosa, Tolliver thought, often ending up at his shop. Strangers meant business for the town's only gunsmith or they meant gun play in the main street or in the saloon. It never failed. Often it was both, at times in rapid succession.

Now, twice inside of a week, two strangers to Tascosa had ridden into town without so much as a hoopla or a private salute from an ordinary citizen. Tolliver, on the porch of his shop, enjoying the sun on his face for a few minutes each day, had noticed them as he noticed every move that went on about him. That awareness had arisen as a scout for the army, out ahead of the troops at a great distance, and first in the line of trouble. He had paid his dues to sit and enjoy the sunlight, finesse a trigger's mechanism in a pistol, set a gun sight to perfection for the nerveless hand, or heart. His own images, his own history, leaped on him in a stab at penance: loose youngster with choice weapons, army scout, shootist, deadly shootist, tired shootist, gunsmith, Tascosa businessman.

Forsythe appeared to Tolliver's practiced eye to be lean, deadly lean, deadly quick, and deadly accurate. It was his manner in the saddle; surprise would never catch him.

Pawkins, he thought, looked as if he never ate, didn't need food, feeding instead on the challenge of the gun, the dare of the taunt, the inky headlines in small newspapers spread across the territory.

Tolliver wondered if there was any difference beside life and death. He'd watch Forsythe and Pawkins like it was a stage play. He'd keep his eye on the main characters. The decision brought him to the saloon in the early evening to watch the early action, the pace setting in motion, the establishment of ploys and characteristics freely given as if posed.

"Hey, Judah," he said to Pawkins in the saloon, "I just missed you one night in Gatesville when I got out of town in a hurry." They were standing at the bar, a few regulars between them, the regulars drifting away in a matter of seconds as the conversation continued.

"I heard you were there, Tolliver," Pawkins said, the name said with respect. "I wondered why you left, but guess it was for the best." He seemed to be saying, "You were older then and older now." His eyes had not stopped shifting around the room, measuring, detecting, assuming nothing.

"Hell, man, I was slower then than I am now, and now I'm almost useless."

"You still have the long fingers and the good hands for fixing these things?" He pointed, from up high, down at his hip-slung weapons.

Tolliver appreciated the message in that movement as did every man in the room experienced in gun play. "Yep, still keep my hand in it." He smiled with his answer, holding out his steady hands, not a twitch in them. "No weight to drag them down."

He added, "Save some time for me, Tolliver. I'll drop in to see you." Tolliver could feel at his fingertips the trigger mechanisms in Pawkins' six guns being tuned so fine that a breath of cool air might set them off. He held his breath for a few seconds.

From the table near the door, Forsythe, not to be left out of the talk, said, "Tolliver, I saw you in Clancy's Place once over in Caliber Pass, just before it burned down. That time when Hostetler was running away with half the towns around and half the women in them, like he was a god from way up in the Nations."

"He did swing a steady trail, didn't he?" Tolliver offered. His head nodded several times and all the men in the room, including Pawkins and Forsythe, looking as if they wondered about the possibilities of such a life, short as it was, but somehow sweet as a pie.

71

Forsythe jumped right back. "Boy could have been dead before he died."

All the men laughed, and Pawkins said, "Until that stagecoach woman, hiding the gun in her skirts, gutted him right up close, him getting so close to her he got too far away."

The banter went on for most of the evening, and the next evening. Some gents who were not there the first night began to drift in, the word spreading about the banter, Tolliver in the mix, Forsythe and Pawkins in the same room, like the place was a loaded canister.

Sooner or later things would happen, the saloon busting up. It was inevitable.

For two nights Tolliver steered the conversation. Others joined in, telling old tales, new lies, their own little actions in the big west. It was a stage play waiting for resolution.

But Tolliver loved it most, at length admitting that he liked Forsythe and Pawkins, knowing how much they reminded him of himself, a mirror dropped beside him as he looked around the saloon, seeing his body in more than one place. The experience was ghost-like, spiritual, and carried more messages than Tolliver could interpret.

"But I like those two gents," he kept saying to himself.

Tolliver meanwhile waited the tip-off, the slightest move. He kept watch. It would be an arched eyebrow, the twitch of a lip, the sweat seeping off a brow so subtle only a candle light or oil lamp could make it visible. The longer the evenings wore on, the longer the shadows grew in the saloon until all shadows were gone. The constant and enjoyable talk stayed at a sense of justice, disarmament. It was tolerable times for Tascosa's saloon life.

Once, in a near silence that slipped into the saloon wolf-like, Tolliver heard the musical bells of a lead ram of a sheepherder's flock. Things were changing, and perhaps duels and gunfights, the kind he had known for years, were also on the way out. More than once he heard the bells in the middle of the saloon, like a knell settling on him, settling on a way of life that was making a final statement.

Yet something told him the climax between Forsythe and Pawkins was coming, within a day or so. Fate said they had been pointing at this day and also said he'd be in the mix, being the gunsmith, being the old and the new in one frame.

So it was that both gunslingers came to the old gunslinger turned gunsmith, leaving their weapons for fine tuning so delicate it could not be measured. Each one, leaving his guns about an hour apart, saying, "I'll be back late afternoon. Make 'em good." The words were almost exact. Tolliver knew the signs.

72

So it spilled over that evening after two rounds of drinks, when an eyebrow twitched or a sneer was instant punctuation to another's words, that the dare was dropped like a gauntlet in the midst of men folk in the saloon. It went outside in a hurry, the regular customers leaving the saloon first, crowding the doorway en masse to get a good viewing spot. The duelists went out last, in turns, like actors going on stage. The evening sun was cut in half by a mountain range, so Forsythe and Pawkins lined up north and south, lest one man get caught in a sun flash.

The silence was the breath ready to set off the trigger mechanisms.

Down the street, at the livery, a horse caught at attention. From the mountain holding half the sun, a wolf called dominion. A twist of dust swirled from the road bed and slipped down an alley like boys at tag. Horse chatter came again, but folk chatter was caught up in dry throats. The curious were here, not because they wanted to see a shooter die, or a shooter lose a duel, but they didn't want to miss whatever might happen.

It all went as planned … almost.

Not one person in town, including the editor of *The Tascosa Herald*, could recall later how it ticked down to the draw of the two shooters. But there came again the melancholy call of the wolf off a rise in the shadows of the mountain. A horse, down an alley beside the livery, kicked at a water trough. The thud was unique and solid. A careless man sneezed in the depths of the crowd.

And the two men, without a word, went for their guns. With grace and speed their hands were full of guns. Each aimed at the other and nerves tensed on triggers at the most sensitive point of balance.

Nothing happened.

The trigger mechanisms clicked again as if they had found empty chambers.

Nothing happened.

Pawkins and Forsythe pulled their triggers half a dozen times, both staring at Tolliver standing at the front of the crowd.

Tolliver's hands were slung on his hips as if he stood in judgment of the world, as if he wore an invisible robe. He stood alone, primary and yet susceptible, as others in the crowd backed away from him.

Before anybody moved, before either of the gunfighters said a word, Tolliver yelled at both of them, his voice ringing the way it might sound coming half wild but controlled from Sunday's pulpit, a strange mix for the former gunfighter turned gunsmith.

"Both of you gentlemen would be dead right now and we'd all go back into the saloon and start drinking again, every damned one of us here. Today would go away and tomorrow would go away on top of it and you'd be forgotten in a hurry." He snapped his fingers with the sound of doom.

"You'd be gone as fast as that." He snapped them again. "Each of you."

Those words settled on everybody in hearing distance, each listener gagged by the weight of truth as the dead-earnest saucer of silence sat down on top of Tascosa.

Still the judge at judgment day, like a prophet off the dark mountain, Tolliver pointed at both of them and began laughing the way he'd laugh at a good story at a saloon rail bar or at a campfire out on the plains.

With that laughter realization settled on all those gathered: Tolliver, in a gesture of mercy, had truly fixed the guns of Forsythe and Pawkins.

He laughed long and loud as he began to saunter toward them, and yelled loudly and clearly, in the same voice of deliverance, its timbre deep with conviction and truth and certainty that no man can deny, "Dead men can't laugh," he said. "Dead men can't drink this night with us. Dead men can't play a decent game of poker with trail pards. Dead men can't saddle up in the morning and ride out on the prairie with the cows. Dead men can't be lovers or fathers." He held both his hands in the air and finished by saying, "Dead men can only swim in the darkest river their minds can imagine."

In the midst of certain truths, the inevitable ones, the humor came to them all, to the duelists and the crowd as a throaty laugh engulfed the whole town of Tascosa in a night that was remembered into two more centuries.

Even the proposed duelers entered into the laughter as they all followed Tolliver the gunsmith back into the saloon.

Falcon Eddie

The two men had stepped from behind the barn with guns drawn and aimed at the family of cowman Jiggs Marion, sitting on the porch of their ranch house. Marion sat beside his wife Merle and their daughter Alva and son Eddie sat on the steps. Alva was nine years old and Eddie was soon to be fourteen.

The men were hatless, wore no gun belts, and blood was evident on the shirts of both men, looking as if they had escaped from prison somewhere in the territory and had a bad run of it.

"Don't move," one man said. "All we want is some food and a couple of horses. We won't hurt anybody if you just do as we say. No tricks. No going for your guns." He was pointing at Marion's side arms. "Throw them down, mister. We won't hurt anybody."

Jiggs Marion threw his guns on the ground.

His wife said, "I'll get you some food. It's still on the table." She stood up.

"No funny stuff. No tricks," the talker said again. "We got your kids here." He looked at Jiggs and said, "And your old man."

"I'm not stupid, mister, and I'm no gun slinger. I'm a cook. I'll feed you, but don't hurt anybody. That won't help you." It seemed to say, in a quick change of her tone, "But it sure will hurt you if I have anything to say about it."

"Go ahead," the talker said, and added, "get us a couple of sombreros, and a couple of canteens, full ones."

Eddie stood up and said, "I'll get the sombreros and the canteens, Mum," he said. "But they don't get 'my' Stetson." His voice came haughty, arrogant.

The other man, looking riled a bit, said, "What's so special about 'your' Stetson, kid? You think you're special? I don't. Go get me your Stetson."

Eddie looked a bit shamefaced, as he said, "I have a bird on my hat. It's mine and it's special."

The intruder was rankled and said, "Go get me your damned Stetson, kid, and no funny stuff. Where is it?"

"It's in my room."

"You got your own room, huh? Nice stuff, kid. I had my own room, too. In jail." He laughed loudly, and then said, "Go get it. Remember, I'm lookin' down the barrel at your kid sister. Don't be too brave."

Eddie Marion went and brought back his Stetson. There, on the top, sat a stuffed bird, brown and white and a bit stippled with spots. It did not

75

look ludicrous.

Eddie handed the man his Stetson.

"Damn, kid," he said in amazement, "I like it. I really like it. It's kinda classy." He put it on and said to his companion, "How's it look on me, Trig? Classy? Think people will remember me in this hat?" He laughed long and loud, and then said, as Mrs. Marion brought food from the kitchen piled across a bread board, "Go get the canteens, kid, with fresh water in them."

Jiggs Marion, who often had questions about his son's role in life, did not give off the smile that tempted his whole face as he watched Eddie go toward the well and past the cage sitting at the end of the house. He saw his son lean against the cage.

The folks who knew him best called him Falcon Eddie. He was born on the Three Rivers Ranch in west Texas of parents who raised and drove cattle for a living. His father, Jiggs Marion, was a brawny, tough cowboy who had come out of Arkansas as a young man, at age 19 and rambunctious; his wife Merle, and Falcon Eddie's mother, was the first girl Jiggs Marion ever knew, and he stole her from the second floor of the Bright Range Saloon in Mount Pleasant, East Texas, on his way west. The posse never caught up to the pair, who made their final escape by floating downstream between two logs, right past the posse camp in early evening. Merle, even before that escape, was in love with the first man who had given her full respect.

Falcon Eddie, without any name for his first three days of life, was given the name Eddie, which was the name of Merle's brother, Eddie Seibers. Neither one ever saw the other.

The Falcon part of his name came some years later when, to his parents concern, and initial regret, he showed no interest in cattle or ranching. His full attention on falcons came when, as a boy, he saw a falcon dive from the clouds to snare a bird in flight. The speed, accuracy, and daring reduced the lad to awe, wonder and total interest only in falcons.

While other boys his age, about ready to get into working ranks on family spreads, were mostly interested in fast draws and fast horses and quick visits to town, Eddie was enamored of prairie falcons and the occasional peregrine falcons, which now and then came into his view. Prairie Falcons were slimmer and longer-tailed than Peregrine Falcons, and looked to be more active and more aggressive in their hunting.

"I can't explain it all the way," Eddie once said to best pal Powell as they sat out on the prairie grass waiting for falcons to dive out of the sun, "but they are so fast that my heart leaps up to meet them. They dive down on other birds like lightning has lit them up. Nothing in the world is as fast as them. Nothing. They are the fastest things in all of creation. One old Indian, from the canyons where the Pueblos are, told me that falcons are messengers from Tinami, god of the heavens, the big chief who sends all his creatures down to us, for however best we can use them."

Powell said, "What was the name of that Indian? Is he the old one with the long scar down his face, like he was hit with a sword?"

"That's him. Why? Ykchen is his name." Eddie said it like he was in the fold of the tribe. "That's his name in the language." The words came out as supporting information, as if he was telling a secret.

Powell, understanding they were swapping precious information, said, "My grandfather says he's the one he'd trust the most because he knows the most secrets and must have earned them ... how to tell a cow is sick before he falls down, or a deer or a sheep ... or where the bear hides in the snow ... or when the big snow is going to come or the wind that makes the sky dark all day. Says he knows all that stuff like it comes to him when he needs it."

Eddie said, "Where do you think that all comes from?"

Powell pointed overhead, "I bet it comes from the same place your falcons come from, from up there."

"I knew it the first time," Eddie said. "It does not let go, like the claws they have, like traps that are as good as steel."

The two pals had been waiting for hours for such an event at that precise moment happened overhead as a falcon dove out of the sky to snare a bird in straight flight across the prairie running off for miles to the mountains. A clutter of feathers drifted down the way buckshot might tell on a bird hit in flight.

"Where did he come from, Eddie?" Powell said in amazement, looking off to the mountains and then overhead again.

"Not just the sky," Eddie said, following the drift of feathers. "They don't live on stars or planets or on the moon." He pointed to the mountains sitting across the wide prairie and past the great river. "They come from up there. Way up. Some day I'm going up there and catch one or get some eggs from a nest, and then we'll see what happens. I heard about bird men in far places that have trained falcons to grab things right out of the air. One drummer told my father about falcons, how they sit on a man's arm and then go fly after something and come back to the man's arm. Then he puts a hood on their head to keep them quiet, keep them from going after something else, like another bird. He said he could bring a book about them if he ever gets to Chicago or St. Louis again."

"Do they eat what they kill?"

"They must," Eddie said. "That's why they do it. They don't have turkey shoots like we do, for the fun of it. It's different with them, the killing. When I get up there and find a nest, I'll tell you what kind of stuff is left over from their killing meals, if there's anything left."

In less than five years, after a dozen trips up into the mountains, Falcon Eddie, becoming an experienced climber as well, came home with two falcon eggs. He'd climbed almost 1200 feet up the face of a cliff and found the scrape or nest of a prairie falcon, with two eggs sitting there, spotted blue-beige eggs that could have knocked him off the cliff with wonder.

"It's my lucky day," he said aloud, not knowing the day was not over for him, nor was his luck all used up.

He wrapped the eggs in a soft fabric his mother had given him and placed them in a small wicker basket he'd made from a fishing creel and swung the basket onto his back. On the way down the cliff, and on the ride home, he kept them warm and protected. Some of the information that had come to him about falcons had prepared him for this part of his destiny.

Nothing had prepared him for the joy he experienced taking care of his possessions.

Or for what was coming to him.

At the far edge of a fenced section of the Three Rivers Ranch, he came upon a falcon caught up in the fence wire. More than once he had dreamed of such a happening, hearing such things from old timers who had spent their lives on the plains. The bird was caught for good, and would obviously die there on the wire unless it was retrieved from the hard clutches of the wire.

But the first thing that hit Eddie, being this close for the first time ever to a live falcon, was to study the bird, committing much to memory, finding ways to describe him in a journal he kept on falcons. The upper parts of the tangled bird, which he determined to be a prairie falcon and not a peregrine falcon, were grayish-brown in color, with lighter edges along the back feathers. The long tail was brown and had a white tip, and there was darker barring along the outer tail feathers. The throat and under parts of the falcon were whitish and showed long, brown spots. The top and sides of the head were dark, from what Eddie could see in the bird's escape attempts. He locked up an image in his mind of the face that had light eyebrows, white cheeks, and a narrow brown mustache above the beak.

Into his journal it would all go.

He wondered if it was the same bird he had seen a number of times on flat wings in stiff, shallow powerful beats, his tail spread, shooting across the prairie chasing squirrels, lizards, prairie dogs and other birds. Every time he had seen such a creature, he'd known a catch in his throat.

But Falcon Eddie, putting his bandana over the bird's head and knotting it in place, subdued the agitated bird. Even with the wings motionless, Eddie knew he had in his hands the fastest creature in the world. The weight was light, but the promise was prodigious. Inserting his catch carefully into the holding sleeve of his jacket, he carried the falcon home with him.

In that manner he brought the bird back to the ranch, like a treasure retrieved, and elation was all over his face as he rode up to the front of the ranch house, where his parents greeted him.

"Is that really a falcon you have, Eddie," his mother said. The glee on his face was answer enough for her.

He showed her the eggs. "We'll have to keep them warm, and we'll have to fix the bird's wounds. He was caught up in the fence wire."

The falcon, keeping the eggs warm, waiting for them to hatch, mended quickly and was trained by Eddie in exhaustive sessions. The first found eggs, it is sad to say, failed to hatch, but Eddie Marion had a role for himself cut out in life. The family admitted that he would never be a cattleman. But he caught a few more falcons, raised a few falcons hatched from eggs taken from cliff tops, and found himself, one day down the line, filling a couple of canteens with water for two bad hombres who had guns trained on his family.

All the training, both ways, came into play.

Falcon Eddie whistled once, and the falcon in the cage with the door now ajar flew up in a quick spiral, exciting everybody. They all stared upward. The bird whirled high in the air, turned over on its back, and with phenomenal speed that neither of the intruders had over seen dove down and snatched the stuffed bird off Falcon Eddie's Stetson. One man ducked for cover and the other, afraid to be target for the bird a second time, dropped his weapon and threw his arms over his head.

And Jiggs Marion, still quick on his feet, fast on the move, snatched his pistol from the ground and shot one man still holding a weapon, and stood over the second man, the bird man, grinning.

The young birdman, Falcon Eddie, raised his leather-sleeved arm and the falcon, in a feathering arrest of flight, came down to roost on that raised arm.

The Legend of the Old Man of the West

At the Gila City Saloon that very night, hard-working, long-time rancher in the region Everett Jensen entered to laughter and glee and was hailed not as a new hero of the still wild west but as the wily old man he was.

"Hey, Everett, you old man of the west, how'd you figure on all that stuff today?" said one man at the bar, nodding his head in a salute and, with a broad grin on his face, offering up a glass of whiskey.

Jensen sipped the offered drink. "Well, Harry, you don't hang around out here for 50 years and not learn something. If it looks like you're not learning anything, better move on to someplace else. And you better not take 50 years to learn that much because you won't last that long in the first place." Jensen showed his run at age with his gray hair that twirled over his ears, the long years of saddle-riding and sun-beating on his face, and a slight infirmity just now touching his left knee, a long-ago throw from horseback. But his blue eyes had not lost a second of clarity, or powers of observation.

"That's nice to hear, Everett, but somethin' has to get in your craw, like it did today, and you gotta know it when it sets in like that, know it for real. How is what I want to know? Does it sit up and growl at you, or simper inward like a pup is whinin'?"

"The way it comes to me, it's the lay of the land, Harry, and the people around you. I saw them pokes just lying there on my way into the bank like there was no reason in the world to take a break so early in the morning. Nothing like the folk I know. None of you gents lays around like that. Not on Friday and Saturday around the corner. You don't have to poke at that from too many angles to get an idea in your head. So, it's like the old coyote or the old wolf of the pack is still learning, and he makes something of something new, or best yield his place in the pack. These gents weren't doing any whittling. They weren't doing any talking. They were just watching, and I figured it was me they were watching, so I just tried an old trick. It's been done before and will be done again, you can bet supper on that. But it worked for me, least until the boys from the Double Ell roped them in. I'd seen them on the way home from town, off in the grass, hassling their cows home.

"You see everythin', Everett, everythin' around you? That way you can't see where yore ridin', can you?"

"You know what it's like, Harry. You've been here a spell too. All you boys have. The thing is I know I can count on all of you. And that's a big difference no matter where or when you're trying o fit in, make a place for yourself." And even as Jensen said it he went back again to the one man in the saloon he had never seen before. In a gray hat, gray vest, long narrow face, pointed chin, drinking his second glass since Jensen had come into the room, and not a smile on his face. Not part of the crowd. Not an old townie. He put the man's face in a secure place in his mind. One never can tell, he thought, even as the whiskey felt clear and gunshot clean in his own mouth, a slight burn down his throat, evening pleasure after a day in the saddle.

He thought about something his father had said, more than 50 years before when they came into the valley on the back end of a wagon, their whole lives piled up in the wagon, and Everett's long, thin, nine-year old legs hanging off the back end like scrawny twigs gathered up in the ride. "Hear me, son, out here it's best to bite the rattler 'fore he bites you."

And there in the corner of his mind, where he lodged and kept important ideas, the words came back to him, in that Tennessee drawl that somehow hung on for the ages, for the long ride: "Hear me, son, out here it's best to bite the rattler 'fore he bites you."

There was no better time and no better reason than to do so this very moment; another part of his mind told him so, even as he went back over the start of this very day, just hours back, as he rode homeward from Gila City.

A strange rider, guns drawn and aimed at him, had come up out of a gulley and faced Everett Jensen. For all his wariness and suspicious circumstances seen over his years, Jensen had been keeping an eye on the trail behind him as he came from Gila City ... and a visit to the bank.

"Horse," he muttered, half disgustedly at his lack of full awareness, "we just got us some mean-looking company. I should have known it. Thought he'd be coming the other way. Could have bet on it."

Earlier in the morning Jensen had mused on a number of things: it was a warm July morning in 1879, and an early touch of air gave its outlook on the day ... the sun would be hot but the breeze would carry a shred of soothing, to be most realized only in evening's balm and delight, after moving a small herd, seeing the branding done, coping with innumerable tasks that made up his life as the owner of a large spread in East Texas. And the streets of Gila City were not yet busy. He had walked out of the Gila City Bank with payroll money for his ranch hands, almost 50 years working the ranch, **J Bar** brand, and had seen too many incidents not to be aware every minute he carried a goodly sum of money.

That's why he casually noticed for the second time two horses at the rail in front of the general store, and two men, obviously their riders, still sitting on the steps as they had when he entered the bank. It was too early in the day for good men to idle on a busy Friday. He stressed his immediate assessment by saying again to himself, "Too early for idling." He made a

81

show of packing a large envelope in his saddle bag, his usual embrace of funds after a bank visit. In the bank some alertness had leaped at him and he had slipped his payroll money inside his Stetson.

Twenty years back in his history, two other men had come out of the trees, at about the halfway point in the ride home, with their guns drawn. That time he was also on the way back to the ranch with wage money after a stop at the bank. The times were a bit notorious and he rode with full alert, including carrying a pistol right on the pommel of his saddle. Both men were surprised when he fired at them, and they fled back into the trees. He did not chase them, but knew he could pick them out of a crowd. Never again did he see them. The story, though, hung on a long time and he couldn't believe how many times it had been told in the Gila City saloons, and elsewhere most likely.

"Hey, Everett," one bar leaner might say, "Tell us agin how you pommel-whipped them poor dumb asses with yore quick-draw from the top of the deck." And he might add, "C'mon, Everett, one more time so's we kin make a legend out of it."

The story might have brought these two newer but still suspicious gents out of the ravine and deep grass that ran right through his fence lines for another mile or so. Neither one of the men had he seen before, and kept his eye on the trail behind him as he rode home. He never saw the third man step from behind a tree with a rifle leveled at his midsection.

"That's one on me," he said, half a joke in his voice, as the rifle slowly moved closer to him. His hands went in the air and the idlers from back in town came right up out of the same ravine, their weapons drawn.

"Get the envelope out of the saddlebag and run off his horse," one of the idlers said.

One tough looking gent, much too heavy in the paunch for a decent day's work on the J Bar, and an odd sense of movement about him as if something was out of joint, climbed down off the saddle and took the envelope from Jensen's saddlebag and stuck it in his own saddlebag. Jensen's horse, smacked hard on the rump, fled across the wide grass.

Jensen put a thought away for future reference: "This gent is the low man on the totem pole in the group because he's uncomfortable yet he's made to climb down from his horse." Later, he would recall saying "Climbed down." It stuck in Jensen's mind. "I'll call him 'Ache," he added, in further classification on which to draw a reference.

"Ache" snugged the saddle bag on his own horse and climbed back up in the saddle with definite signs of full discomfort and the three robbers galloped off.

Jensen realized he might not have much time, so he put his money into an old post hole and stuffed dry grass on down on top and moved off, marking the place indelibly in his mind and began whistling for his horse. As bidden, the horse poked its head up out of a gulley and trotted back. Jensen mounted and fled back toward town as the three bandits, obviously checking on their spoils and knowing they had been played for fools, began their chase.

The old man of the west, Everett Jensen, born to the saddle, expert horseman and rider, having exclusive picks for his own horses, let the big red horse have his wings. Able now to wave his hat, he drove the animal as great speed back down the trail, where his hat-waving and yells alerted other horsemen off the trail. They responded quickly, recognizing a neighbor in trouble. They converged on the trio of bandits, and without a shot fired rounded them into a small herd of distraught and down-faced robbers who had been done in by the old man.

"Take them into the sheriff. Tell him I'll be back tonight. I have to pay off my boys. Some of them will be coming back into town with me tonight."

"Where you going now?" one neighbor asked.

"Back to dig up my money. I buried it back there under some dry grass and have to get it back before some critter moves off with it. These pokes just ran off with an empty money envelope."

The neighbor laughed loudly and slapped his thigh in glee. "Hey, Everett, they shoulda known not to fool around with the old man of the west. He's too smart for all of 'em. We kin start some new stories in the saloon starting right off tonight and these three dudes goin' smack into the new legend. Yessiree, tonight will be a hot time at the old saloon, and these boys'll be looked at like the fools they been, chasin' for nothin' at all. We might have us a parade and march past the jail ahooterin' and ahollerin' to beat the band for those dumb ass pokes who shoulda knowed better than play the old man for a fool." He laughed again and added, "I'll betcha old Dublin Mickey on the piana will make up a new song for 'em, like chasin' air or nothin' in an empty envelope, or three dopes headin' for ropes. Hey, Everett, maybe that ain't too bad if I do say so myself." He laughed loudly again in his own glee, and then asked, "How in hell did you know they was comin' after you, Everett?"

"I'll tell you tonight," Jensen said, who rode back on the trail, found his money and headed back to the ranch as the trio of unsuccessful robbers were herded back to the sheriff and their time in jail, notwithstanding the "three dopes headin' for ropes" still sounding on the neighbor's tongue.

His ride back to the ranch completed, the pay-off made, and supper finished. He set off for the return ride to town with a few hands that had remained behind, knowing he was going back into town and amid a new cause for partying and celebration; any kind of survival in a tough situation in a tough world indeed called for celebration. It was ordinary folks becoming heroes for a short time; it was due respect for wits and wiles. Yet there was no doubt it was the stuff of legends.

No man at the time had a bigger piece of that respect than Everett Jensen.

Now, he was here, leaning at the bar, the stories popping around as usual when something fortunate happened to any one of his many good friends, and the new, strange face in the crowd still looking at him. It was not a sinister face, but it had some edges to it, Jensen decided, edges to which he ought to pay note.

So he turned again to his long-time pal Harry Cruthers and said, "It's always been a rule with me, Harry to be ready for the difference-makers when they come around you, or people you don't recognize." He was looking directly at the stranger as he said that, but shifted his eyes away in a hurry. "I know every man in this room, some of you going back almost the 50 years I've been here. Most of you for 10-12 years or more anyway, and I know I can count on you; what you do, what you might do, and, most important, what you won't do. That's plain and simple to all of us. That's every man in this whole room but one. There's one stranger here I never met, never had the pleasure, so I'd like to buy this stranger a drink if he would come up here and establish a friendship," and he might have added, "Bite the rattler afore he bites you." He nodded at the stranger, who rose from his seat and came to the bar.

"This one's on me," Jensen said. Welcome to Gila City. What brings you here?"

"Just riding through, looking for work in a week or so, but perhaps farther west, at the foot of the mountains. Name's Jode Prescott and nothing special about me. But I appreciate the drink." His eyes did not play tricks on old Jensen, who thought for the second or third time about "biting the rattler 'fore he bit him."

"Well," said Harry Cruthers, "that's one hombre won't sneak up on you, Everett, not without wearin' a mask no how."

The stranger, Jode Prescott, said, "Thanks for the drink. I'm turning in now for an early start. Nice to meet all you considerate folks." He doffed his hat and left. The door swung squeakily behind him to a close.

Another patron said, "Hey, Everett, tell us agin about that lady situation you run into, at that bank in Mesquite."

In the basking light that he ordinarily didn't seek, Jensen realized it was like a special night out for his long-time pals, and some of his own ranch hands, and an enjoyable scene they had all been through before. Nothing more pleased him than being with good friends and having a good time. It was as good as a payday. So he began a new episode.

"I saw this guy in the bank at Mesquite eyeing a lady's folding money as she put it in her little satchel that she carries on her arm. If there was smoke for interest he would have been on fire and shooting off a cloud. I locked his face in place for future reference. Got his name through an encounter with an Oklahoma lawman. I come home and about a week later heard the lady was robbed on the way back to her ranch. So I let the lawman know my suspicions and about a month later, when he was corralled, the lady positively identified him as the robber. Said he knocked her off her seat in her buggy after she found him lying beside the road and stopped to check him out. Not like a real robber, that dude."

"Just the look on his face tipped you? Hell, we all have that when we go lookin' at a roll of bills or a sack of gold dust. Nothin' else to him? No stick-out stuff loose on him? My gawd, Everett, it's like you kin look right through a body and find what makes him move."

And the legend, as it swirled on itself, gathered momentum with additional episodes as Everett Jensen, on his way home in the morning after a night with pals, his spirits as high as the sun bright and laying hands on everything in sight, saw a small reflection of sunlight off the side of the road ahead of him. He dipped his horse down into a gulley, tethered him, grabbed his rifle and backtracked through high grass and brush and climbed a small hillock.

He waited out any movement and after 20 minutes, saw a rider slowly come off the side of the road, from behind a large rock. It was the stranger passing through town from the night before, Jode Prescott. The legend of the old man of the west gathered a new episode when Jensen put a round right over Prescott's head and forced him to dismount. He made him walk all the way back to town, and told the sheriff, "This hombre was about to bushwhack me on the road back to the ranch. Now I can't prove it, but he's got a lot of explaining to do about why he was flashing his rifle from the side of the road, and sort of well-hidden. If I didn't catch the reflection of his rifle, he could have dropped me. Nobody out here wants anybody sitting on the side of the road, hidden, with a rifle in his hands. There is no reason for doing so, so some steps have to be taken in this case. I don't want to spend my time looking for this gent as I come and go."

The sheriff told Prescott, that very evening as he let him out of jail, "I'll say it once, and no more … you git ridin' and ride fast and far and if you ever come within a hundred miles of here I'll drop you myself."

Prescott was never seen again, the legend, of course, grew some more, and Everett Jensen, hardly done compiling the full complement of his history as the old man of the west, plain fell asleep one night in his 87th year and closed the book on it all.

Fisher MacKerell

His father was a jokester, Fisher MacKerell'd say, because the last thing he ever heard from him was a long and deep laugh, the echo of which followed him out of Gloucester harbor not far from Boston all the way to the town of Bush Hill on the Pecos River on the western slope of the Sangre de Cristo Mountains in New Mexico. The year was 1884. He knew the continuous taunt of his name, but stubbornness refused to let him change his name. He allowed only "Fish" to be used as a diminutive settlement. And "Fish" he was to all those who stood on the other side of the bar.

He also only allowed that being so named by his jokester father made him a fast gun with his left hand, after the taunts on his western move forced him to endless practice with his revolver, a Colt with a worn handle starting to wear. The practice lasted all the way across the country, a ride that took him two years of knock-about work at other things "western." He was a drover on a few short drives, a chuck wagon cook for a short spell after an accident to a cook, a blacksmith tenderfoot and a livery man until he knew how to take care of a horse. But he never wore a badge or robbed a bank or stagecoach or worked a bar until Papa Lorenzo offered him a job behind the bar at the Pecos Headwater Saloon near the start of the river.

MacKerell was a decent-looking fellow with wavy blond hair, brows darker than the locks on his head, blue eyes, square chin, and spoke like a professor out for a look around the west.

Home, he found, was behind the saloon bar at Bush Hill. It didn't take the student of men too long to realize the nature of the task; keep the customers happy, keep the boss happy, and enjoy the in-between. He had become, in a short time on the job, a reader of people, a fair and ready arbitrator in minor squabbles, a ready pistol under the bar at the threat of more serious trouble, and a favorite of one of the "ladies of the house," Clara Ridgley. Clara, new in town, new at her assignment, depended on Fish MacKerell to give her both a helping hand and a heads up whenever it was needed.

Clara told some of the working ladies that she thought MacKerell was as handsome as he was kind.

The truth be known, we oftentimes don't know when a story starts or stops in a person's life, or resumes continually like a serial. Such it was with these two characters here, Fish, as he was called, and Clara.

We've had a glimpse at MaKerell's start on things, and Clara Ridgley, from the following revelation, had her life renewal get a kick-start when a freighter found her on the edge of the trail apparently having had the hell beat out of her. She was a bloody mess, her clothes torn in rags, but she clutched a slim stick in one hand, looking as though she had been fighting off her attacker. The freighter brought her to the saloon and Fish MacKerell because he was the most solicitous man he knew in the town he only visited for deliveries and a whistle-wetter if it was the last delivery from his wagon. He accomplished two steps because of Clara Ridgley who made him hurt when he just looked at her.

MacKerell put Clara in his bed in his room, at the back end of the Pecos Headwater Saloon, then summoned the local mid-wife to check Clara and give what help she could until Doc Hansen came into town on a weekly run from down-river. The woman took good care of Clara, got her cleaned up, attired in a proper dress during the day, and sat with her through a few meals and lots of sleep on Clara's part. MacKerell spent his sleeping hours on a few blankets in a corner of the saloon, the light of a bright moon falling through the windows of the saloon, bringing a sense of warmth with it, and a presumption of hope: Clara Ridgley was a most beautiful woman who had totally leapt into the senses of the bartender, who had never been in love.

In the matter of little more than a week, Clara said she wanted to do some work to payback for her tender care, "but not the usual stuff," she also advised. She went to work, at MacKerell's suggestion, in the kitchen behind the bar. As it turned out, she was an excellent cook and soon had a list of customers who extolled her special preparations. "She makes the best pie, cooks a roast better than ever, does wonders with beans and bacon and eggs," they'd say, and carry on about good taste hanging out in the back of the Pecos Headwater saloon.

When the time came, Clara cured and healthy, MacKerell asked her what had happened to leave her alone out of the trail. He made the approach as casual as he could, but Clara saw his minor discomfort.

"Oh, Fish, don't be so easy on me. I can take it, even though it hurts to talk about it. It started with a big man who had no name I ever heard and who held up a stagecoach I was on. He killed the driver and two others and took me along with a strongbox that was up on top of the stagecoach. He even killed one of the horses tied to the one he used to haul the strongbox and me out of there. We got to some hide-out in the mountains before he opened the box. When he found there was nothing there he wanted, he went after me and beat the hell out of me a number of times. I made believe I was sleeping one night when he was drinking, I guess it was about a week later, and when he passed out, I ran off all the horses but took one for myself, and left there. The horse threw me off later on and I wandered a couple of days with just a stick in my hand, and the freighter found me. He was the first nice man I met out here. You're the second. I was on my way to visit my sister in California. But I don't know if I want to go back on the road again. At least, just not now."

Her eyes were soft for the bartender. And they were thrown together in their work, in their interest in each other, and each was able to read the other, neither of whom would try to hide any of their feelings.

So it was a full alert for MacKerell when a big man, noisy at his entrance, and scowling at a customer with his feet sticking in the way as he made his way across the saloon to stand at the bar. He stared at Clara standing at the door to the kitchen with her mouth ajar. With his eyes opened wide, and a sickening grin on his face that quickly turned as mean as a bronc gone bad in a miserable hurry, the big man slammed his fist slammed down on the bar top.

He said to MacKerell, "A bottle of the best, barkeep," he said, "and her," as he nodded at Clara. "She'll do fine and dandy for me. Fine and dandy."

MacKerell, quickly figuring out who the noisy big man was, though not by name, said, "She's not part of the goods for sale." His voice was in his best Gloucester coast English, and noticeably said directly at the big man and not as an aside. "The lady is not part of any of the goods in this establishment. You better understand that right from the start."

The big man, not alarmed by the bartender with a voice different from what he normally heard from a bartender, offered a twist to his words. "We go back a time, me and the so-called lady. We got history. Ask her and she'll tell you or I'll make her tell you what she's done for me in the past." He slammed his fist down on the bar and said, "Off the top shelf or what you got hidden down under the bar. The best stuff. I'm gonna celebrate findin' my old friend."

He yelled across the room. "Hey, you, get over here now. We got business to take care of." He slammed the bar top again to reinforce his demand.

"Don't move, Clara," MacKerell said. "Stay right where you are. Big Mouth here isn't going to bother you anymore and as soon as the sheriff gets here we're going to ask him to check out that stagecoach robbery down to Elsmore where even a horse was killed by the robber. We know there are two witnesses who can testify against the man who did it."

When the big man swung around, hand going for his gun, he found the bartender had a Colt no more than 6 inches from his eyes, and dead center between his brows. He could see the weapon was fully loaded.

"I'd love you to go for the gun, mister," MacKerell said. "Make this a great day. Do it up good for me, the man who beats up a lady, the man who shoots a horse because he can't get the leather loose, the man who shoots a poor old traveler who doesn't even carry a gun. Draw that weapon.

Please do so." The bore of the revolver was steady in the big man's eye.

The big man went as soft as an old grape. He went diminished. His mouth was wide open in surprise as the Colt sat in his eyes as steady as the evening star. The bartender, he swore, was not breathing, and did not blink his eyes.

The Bush Hill sheriff rushed in the door. "What've you got there, Fish, a plain big mouth I just heard about, or what?"

MacKerell said, "You have a poster about a big man that robbed the stage down Elsmore way, killed a passenger who was not armed, an old man, and shot a horse, one of the coach horses, shot him dead on the spot still in his traces." He pointed to the big man. "This is him." Clara will testify to that. He beat the hell out of her before she was able to get away from him."

At that moment, Clara came straight from the kitchen doorway and said, "He killed the driver, Sheriff. Killed a poor old passenger. Killed the poor horse. And he beat the hell out of me and I want to beat him back."

She rushed at the big man who ducked as she flew at him, and he went for his gun again.

Fisher MacKerell, one time Gloucester resident, supposedly bound to the sea from birth, beat him to the gun with a shot that almost tore his hand from the pistol grip.

The sheriff whacked the big man on the back of his head with the butt of his gun, dropping him in a double agony, blood loose as well as his screams.

MacKerell was over the bar and held Clara Ridgley in his arms. She was crying hysterically.

The succeeding trial was to be held within the week, as the other witness was called from Elsmore to appear at the Bush Hill trial. And the big man's name was finally revealed; Lester Goodfry, a known killer from Missouri, who had escaped two incarcerations in two different facilities, one in Missouri and one in Kansas.

Goodfry was in the Bush Hill jail, in a cell across from the town drunk who had been locked up for his own good after threatening another customer at the saloon. The drunk said, "I heard you got shot by that Eastern cowboy, the fisherman from way back on Atlantic beaches. That sure don't say much for you as a big killer, not from what I heard. He probably couldn't have even shot you anyway if he pulled the trigger in your face. Probably would have missed by a mile. Bartenders don't make good gunmen."

"I'll get him soon as I break out of here. This place is a cinch to beat. If you shoot off your mouth about it, I'll shut your mouth forever." He wrung his hands together and said, "I'll twist your neck like this and your legs'll be shaking long after you're gone dead in my hands."

The drunk, favored often with a free drink by MacKerell, a free meal on the sly from the kitchen, smiled as he rolled over and went to sleep for one more night of his own incarceration, knowing this stay was also arranged by his pal Fish. He slept easily, even as Goodfry was hatching up his plan.

The drunk heard nothing in his pleasant sleep, even as Goodfry was at the lock on the cell with a piece of metal, strangely shaped, he had drawn from one of his boots in the darkness. The deputy on duty was knocked sideways by Goodfry, who hit him until he was unconscious. Then Goodfry retrieved his weapon belt from a hook on the wall, his pistol still in the holster, and took a rifle from the rack. Slipping out of the jail in near darkness, he mounted the deputy's horse, rode slowly down beside the jail and out of town.

The sheriff, in early morning, rushed into the Pecos Headwater Saloon and called MacKerell from the rear. "He broke out, Fish. Sometime this mornin', before sunrise. He got out of his cell, banged up Arty Swalen pretty bad and took his horse. He got his own guns from the jail. He's comin' back, Fish, you gotta know that. He's the type will sneak back in here and shoot you behind the counter or in your bed, and maybe go after Clara. There'll be hell goin' on here, and you know it."

"No there won't, Sheriff," MacKerell said. "Just put out the word that I'm going out to look for him. I'll do that. You know I can beat him. He doesn't know that. You just make sure Clara doesn't get hurt. That's all I ask."

The town was quiet all that day and well into the night. The moon, on its last legs, made a low trip on the horizon. Night creatures signified their presence with ownership calls or searching calls out across the grass, the calls going down the Pecos until they failed in darkness. The owl in the livery made a hit on a mouse, only its wings heard by a few horses. The mouse was not heard from.

A single light was on in the sheriff's office, all the cells empty, when Fish MacKerell mounted a big gray at the livery, assured the rifle was sheathed in the saddle, and rode out of town. On his belt he wore the revolver that he had come west with, the Colt with the handle worn down to dread comfort.

The sun found MacKerell well out of Bush Hill, the river sitting off to his right as he headed east. A range of small hills and hummocks sat out in front of him, like bread dough piled up for baking. The horse was an easy rider and the low rays of the sun hit his face and felt comfortable on his skin.

Aloud he said, "It's a good morning for a shoot-out, Mr. Goodfry.

90

I'm here hoping you will oblige me."

He put his arms out beside him in a gesture that said he was welcoming the day, saying hello to the prairie and the mountains and the river and the sun aloft in its promise. A great part of his early life came rushing back to him and heard his father's laughter and his great voice around the cracker barrel in the old bait house and he saw the sails out in the harbor and on the rim of the ocean where the whales and sharks and the real mackerel swam by the thousands, and he felt the keen breeze coming off the water as it comes to a person from no other place else in the world, but he was not unhappy where he was. Clara was here. He thought he'd been looking for her forever; and she was here, waiting for him to come back to town.

A sense of good comfort rushed back into his whole body to take its place again and he began to sing an old sea ditty, the only song he could remember from home:

"Fifteen men on a dead man's chest
Yo ho ho and a bottle of rum
Drink and the devil had done for the rest
Yo ho ho and a bottle of rum.
The mate was fixed by the bosun's pike
bosun brained with a marlinspike
And cookey's throat was marked belike
It had been gripped by fingers ten;
And there they lay, all good dead men
Like break o'day in a boozing ken
Yo ho ho and a bottle of rum."

He sang it a few times, nodded his head as though locked into the song, attention-grabbing, though his eyes continually searched for movements, surprises on the horizon, or creatures disturbed from their places of rest.

And there, off to the right, between him and the curl of the river showing off to the right, a tree moved. He looked elsewhere, came back to the spot, saw it had moved again, saw it was not a bear, saw it was not a wolf, saw it was not a tree.

Everything said it was Goodfry sitting like a bushwhacker in a hidden place, but obviously moving around to get a better position for his attack.

The once-destined fisherman, confirmed westerner, bartender, student of people, a hopeful lover of a lovely lady, studied the land, thought about moves, made a plan on the instant.

With a quick tug on the reins, he drew the gray to a halt, dismounted and bent one foreleg of the horse as if to study its hoof. For a minute he studied the hoof and shoe, touched it a few times, set it back on the ground, stood solicitously and patted the horse on the neck, as if to say he was sorry the gray was hurting. He led him off the trail, down into a woody swale where a few trees were clustered.

Knowing he was out of sight of Goodfry, he hastened to the bank of the river, closer to him now than earlier, ran along the banking and kept out of Goodfry's sight. When he found a defensible position, he halted his advance, gained his breath and sat to wait out the villain lying in wait.

It did not take long to wait out the impatient bushwhacker, who took leave of his position and squirreled his way down the river bank from tree to rocky mound to tree and swale until MacKerell heard him about 30 or so yards away from his position.

MacKerell, suddenly standing, caught Goodfry in an unwary position, half turned to him, looking at a boater downstream yelling at someone on the far banking.

Goodfry, aware in an instant that he was not alone, turned quickly and saw the innocuous, wise-eastern bartender standing and facing him, his left hand hovering in a position to draw his weapon.

Goodfry laughed. "I heard you was comin' for me, so now you got me. Whatcha gonna do? Shoot me like you didn't the other day. Gonna draw down on me, barkeep with the funny words?"

"You afraid to draw on me, bushwhacker? Were you sitting out here like a snake ready to jump me when I wasn't looking, catch me not paying you mind? Do you think me that stupid to play games with you?"

His hands continued their steady position in place to draw, left-handed, his Colt revolver with the handle worn smooth.

High overhead a hawk screeched on a sudden diversion of its flight. On the river the distant voice of the boater called out again and another man, hidden by some obstruction, answered with an unintelligible retort. The hawk screeched again and dove swiftly down on the grass where a rabbit leaped around to escape capture.

All of it crammed Goodfry with its natural being, which transferred itself to an immediate thought that maybe the bartender fit the scene better than he had reckoned.

Desperately he went for his weapon, and knew the swift and terrible realization that he had not gotten off his own shot before one hit him high on the chest. He died staring up to the sky and seeing the rabbit struggling in the clutches of a deadly hunter.

High Canyon Deadlock

Bart Mastiff lowered his rifle off the top of the stone rim and sat back on the rocky ground. Sweat poured off his brow, his back ached, and the sun seemed to reach its fingers into each extremity of his body. Trying to continually advise himself to accept the pain, he was twisted in position, the one wound having seeped two days of redness at his side where the dry remnant toasted in the sun. Two days without water and he knew they were near the end of the trail, both him and his nephew Mark, also wounded, lying a dozen yards away. They had been delivering the deed to his niece's little ranch to the district land office when they had been jumped.

The tongue in his mouth felt like an old sponge long from water. He could count the cracks in the roof of his mouth, his swollen tongue doing the arithmetic. Not a shot had been fired at them in over four hours in the canyon siege and he could not figure out why the bushwhackers' tactics had changed. They easily had the upper hand, and canyon shadows shifted with unseen ease around them, providing an assortment of cover.

He thought of the young Indian he had found a few years earlier in one of these canyons, a small group of peccaries snorting too close, the smell of blood in the air, the Indian boy alone and in pain. Bart wasn't sure if this was the same canyon, but assented that they all looked alike; dead ends often holding darkness or mystery, sheer walls touching the sky, ground unbearably dry and hard, creatures that moved as sly as shadows against dark backgrounds. Even at high noon there could be dark shadows on one side of the canyon or the other, depending on how enormous heat or ice sleds had been at work in their early formation. Out here it was easy for a man to get lost. He had been lost when he found the young brave unarmed, dry as tinder, blood clotted on his backside, lying against the canyon wall. He had tended him for three days, feeding him, tending the wound, being generally alert in such a predicament. When he woke on the third bright morning he found himself in the midst of a party of tribesmen. After talking with the young one, they had carried the boy off with them, but had left Bart a pouch of water, a slice of dry meat, and his weapons put down on the ground about a hundred yards away, allowing him notice of their act, full payment for his deed.

Silence reigned out and beyond, the high canyon and the silence both lounging about like a blanket much too big for its task. The outlaws, whoever they were but obviously from town and in someone's pay, had changed their scheme of attack. Two days earlier they had surprised him and his nephew Mark on the trail, four shouting, shooting, desperate men, jumping at them and almost getting them in their clutches. But Big Red,

93

Bart's horse, had barreled through their minute blockade, with Mark's roan in close pursuit. There was no doubt that Big Red was the best horse west of the Mississippi, and Mark's mount, Shady Pal, was not far behind. They had got to a defilade position among the rocks of the canyon wall after a desperate run to safety. One canteen had been punctured by a round, the second one out there somewhere, dropped on the ride to partial safety.

Bart counted the rounds in his belt. He had seven left, and a full clip in his revolver. Mark had not as yet fired off one shot.

Bart looked over at Mark, behind another boulder, his shirt deeply stained, blood most likely dried up at a shoulder wound. Bart knew he'd be little help to him now, physically or mentally. Even without his wound, Mark provided too much slack with his mousy voice, his outlook on life in general, and his place in it in particular, as though he was forever lost in all that was around him. There were times, even as kids, that Mark had lost a fight before it had started.

"We'll never get out of here, Bart," he said again, the near-whimper prevalent in his words. "They have us cornered. It's best we do what they'll ask, I can feel it. They'll let us go, once they got the deed in their hands. It's what they came after. You and I both know that." Bart knew Mark'd never have a second thought if he lost his sister's spread. That's why the deed, yet to be registered at Bola City, was in his shirt pocket, the blood perhaps already atop the signature.

Bart could see his niece Sally on the porch of the small house, the two children at her side, their anxious eyes often out on the trail for their father, gone six months now on the drive with the herd, and the only message had been the delivery of the deed to the small spread, won somewhere north of them in a poker game. They'd been a short time on the ranch when the rider who had left the herd to deliver the precious piece of paper, had shot off his mouth about his part in the small drama. Like all small talk in all small towns, stories and assumptions grew about true ownership of the spread, a possible crooked game, an improbable draw to an inside straight, and questions about what else was in the kitty to match the deed. Sally was only too aware of how her husband could be overcome when cards were in his hands. If he bet the herd and won the deed, chances are that he'd bet it again. Each dawn the silence, the questions and the doubts pounced on her. "Bart," she had said one evening, "the kids and me count on you a lot more than you realize." Bart knew she had said a whole mouthful, and more, in those few words.

As in a true difference, Mark called out again from his spot in the shadow of a huge chunk of stone fallen from the rim of the canyon. "Bart, ought we throw up a white flag, let them know we're willing to talk? There might just be some worth to all the chatter we heard back there, about ownership and cheating. Why should we have to pay for it like this?"

Bart Mastiff wondered about genes in the family, how Mark must have been cheated on his supply. He wanted to scream out at his nephew, but it would add nothing to their comfort or safety and might easily excite the four bushwhackers. Once more he heard little but silence, saw minor shadows move on the ground and against the canyon wall, counted his bullets one more time. The sun was higher, it seemed, and hotter, and his mouth began another slow torture as he tried to swallow a bit of spittle; he could not find a spot of it.

None of the bushwhackers was known by him. He was sure of that, and yet wondered who might have hired them to collect the deed. Mark whined again, sounding like an animal in a trap. Bart, on the spot, further discounted him as any possible help. He snuck a look out across the canyon, and then up and down the fissure that it was. Nothing moved. There was total silence. He did not even hear a bird call, or any cry or sound from an animal of the area. He felt like he was alone in the world. But that was not so. They were probably waiting for him to dry into tinder, die in the sun. And they might even be drinking out of Mark's canteen at the very moment. He peeked again, over the edge of the rock. Again he saw stillness, if you can see it; heard silence if you can hear it; felt life on the edge, if you can feel it. He was only aware of some transition at hand, some mystery beyond his knowledge.

Even to those who listened to him later, he swore he heard the arrow on the air. He didn't see it; he heard it, a whistle in it, a simple whoosh of parting air the way lips purse up at a good whistle. The arrow struck the ground about ten feet from him. Then one landed directly between Mark and him. Still, he had seen nothing, no one, no bowman of any description. Moments later, a third arrow, in a more direct flight, hit the rock face ten or twelve feet directly above him and clattered to the ground exactly behind him. It was two feet away, the arrow head broken off, the shaft yet smooth and almost polished.

He saw, again, nothing. No one. No shadow. No silhouette. No sprung bow.

And then the reality of it all hit him, as he realized the four desperadoes most likely had not seen any shadow at all, but had felt some scourge come among them, come over them, right from the heart of canyon silence.

Chigger Boom and the Night the Devil Broke Loose

Lots of folks down in south Texas still tell the story of the relentless search for one most prized horse stolen down Rancho Lobo way. They tell the story even years after the horse was stolen during the night of one of the greatest storms that ever roared in from the Gulf of Mexico. Like Hell was shot out of a cannon, they said of that storm, and calling it "The Night the Devil Broke Loose." The winds, roaring like wild steam engines, ripped inland from the Gulf and cut a scandalous path of devastation more than 80 miles wide. Roofs of barns sailed in the air like wings of ungodly giant birds, windows in meager huts imploded before their scanty roofs came free. One small settlement not very far from Rancho Lobo saw every one of its buildings blown apart the way dynamite could do it. And the horse, a 6-year old stallion, a prized animal from the first day, went by the name of Chigger Boom and belonged to 16-year old Chuck Curtin, the son of a rancher.

That's going too fast for some folks, I'd guess, so we'll have to go back to just about the beginning when Chigger Boom came into the world of Texas, near the grass town called Rancho Lobo that lasted almost 50 years, but folded up one night and died a sudden death in another Gulf storm.

But that is beside the real story.

So, we go to the very beginning of the tale of Chigger Boom: On the wobbliest legs imaginable, resembling a bean pole ensemble, the foal managed to stand erect for the first time, and on the first attempt this day, with a bare breath in the air coming right off the grass as if it was squeezed directly from a flask. The excitement, so alive, climbed right up the two walls of the barn, and could have ignited the dry wood. Chuckie Curtin, barely grown himself, he too rail-slim from a meager diet of beans and bread and coffee thin as spit, marked the character of the colt with a demonstrative question, leaping in the air as he said to his father: "Ain't he something, Dad?" They were standing in the idea of a barn, open on two sides to the weather, and not a nail left for pounding on the entire property.

The colt, on this first day, made tears come to Chuckie's eyes. "He's all mine, Dad? All mine? I ain't never been so lucky. Call me Lucky Chuckie if you want. I'll answer." His father said he was growing the way he had, "like being 11 one day and forever old the rest of the way." It was him saying a whole passel of lessons were picked up in one day of the worldly classroom.

Hollis Curtin, who had brought the colt through a difficult birth, smiled with appreciation and pride in his son and in his own good luck with the colt on this early morning. All troubles seemed insurmountable at first, but Curtin was further graced with simple patience born of a harsh beginning, his own birthright; he'd do what it would take for his only son, his only child, to keep an edge on the tough world, even if it was tenuous at best.

And do the same for the colt. Out here a man's best friend was his horse. Some of his days his memory was long and then short; on other days, it was short and then long. He knew the difference at dawn.

On an early morning of another day, all the way back in the hills of Kentucky, his father had walked over the hill with his rifle over one shoulder, to go off to war. He never returned. That morning came back to him in one vision as clear in his mind as if it was earlier this same day. He had turned and waved, his father, and it was the way some men say goodbye for a long weekend, or goodbye forever. "Long as you can count, it keeps coming," he heard him say.

"What are you going to call this ol' horse, Chuckie?"

"Chigger Boom, Pa. His name's Chigger Boom."

"Where in tarnation did that name come from, son?"

"Well, Pa, I turn things over in my mind all the time, funny sounds and strange sounds and things that sound like music to me but really ain't music. I just heard myself saying 'Chigger Boom,' and that's his name. Can I name him that?"

"He's yours to name, raise, saddle in time, ride forever, if that's what you want, Chuckie."

Hollis Curtin remembered the day, in the back of a wagon on the edge of the grass, when Chuckie was born, and lucky to have someone who loved him from then on. It would be this way with the colt. Here, in the west, on the edge of the wild world, a man and a horse were closer than twins. The pair, when treatment and respect abounded, were abided in both directions, which a man could not get by without a good horse. The sooner a man learned that, the better off he was … and with the horse of his choice. Selection was important as the weapons he chose; one day, or more than one day, such possessions would save his life.

The way things were in the growing west, Chuckie was bound to face such a circumstance. He'd make sure the boy was ready, and the colt, this Chigger Boom, was a grand start for him.

He'd keep his eye on the boy, though he knew well beforehand the care that Chuckie would devote to Chigger Boom. With good care the young horse would be with Chuckie for 20 years and perhaps more. Some cowpokes of his acquaintance, the older gents of the herd crowd, said they heard of good horses with good care living into their 30s and early 40s, though the latter were not working horses for that long. With good care at all times, good food without stinting on it, proper rest at work, some horses were as good as sons, as good as fathers, to their riders. Curtin held that image for his son.

As for Chuckie he saw that spindly foal of the caricatured birth, stride into the colt, always moving toward that target of a stallion from that first day.

"Pa," he said on his own 13th birthday, "ain't Chigger coming along like we knew he would. Some of the boys over at the X-Bar-X have offered to buy him anytime, and each one of them have said it to me secretly like they don't want the others to know they got a real interest in buying him."

"You've done a great job with that horse, Chuckie. He stands out in the whole area. Someday they'll be naming foals after him, like Chigger Miss or Chigger Jack."

"Won't that be something, Pa, and you were the one that brought him through that tough night right at the beginning. It's like he was born by you and given to me and that's as good as it gets for horses."

"The part I like as much as anything is the way you can shoe him. You learned that like you were taught in school from the first day. I know you have something going on there that I haven't picked up yet, but I'm working on it."

"Oh," Chuckie said, sort of surprised and yet excited, I got it fixed, Pa, so that I can find Chigger no matter where he goes. I could trail him right over Mount Constable and down the other side to the river."

"Long as someone don't have to change his shoes, huh?"

"Oh, Pa, you knew all along."

"I knew something but I haven't picked up the sign yet, though I sure did study it for a spell. It's got to be pretty tricky, like you invented something new." For a long moment he studied his son, and then he said, "You worried about stealing, Chuckie? Like somebody stealing Chigger?"

"It scares the heck out of me, Pa. Chigger's like my brother, he's my pard, and we're best friends. It's the way it's supposed to be and I'm doing what I can to keep it that way. He's almost five years old now and he's all horse. I swear he is." He stared at the horse across the corral and loved the great lines of strength and muscle that moved under his black coat. Chigger snickered as if he knew the attention being paid to him. The sun bounced in waves off his coal black coat like sheen off a pond face. In turn, the fence line beyond Chigger Boom seemed miniature in comparison to the great horse like he was a blaze of quiet energy.

"Do you see what I mean, Pa? Or hear it?"

Impressions were all over the elder Curtin as he studied this son of his. "You've won me over on all this, Chuck." It was probably the first time Curtin had called his son by the grown-up version of his name, as if it had been earned, and wondered if the boy had missed it.

But Chuck Curtin looked at his father and said, "Thanks, Pa."

A few nights later, as the story goes in most all quarters where it's been told, Hell came right up out of the Gulf and dropped itself on the whole area, with Rancho Lobo in the middle. The storm rode in with the darkness at the end of a nice, peaceful cowboy's day and the beginning of a night of terror and destruction, the wind roaring like the very demons it called upon, a howling and a force loose upon the land the way curses are administered, man and his property as fair game for the furies loosed.

The full bang of the storm hung over the land for the longest 12 hours in some people's lives. Five people were lost without any trace of their departure, and others were hurt so badly it took months to get well again. Cattle herds were driven far apart, some never fairly reclaimed, and many barns and homes sustained damage that would take weeks to repair, if at all possible.

With the weariness of knowing that a bad element was always about in quick, new towns, there came at the same time of the storm those thieves and scoundrels of all makes and types looking for "the free stuff," things gone loose somehow in the storm and therefore up to claim, as if "the free stuff" had been abandoned at sea like a foundering ship, with any interpretation of claim due for argument.

People in the town of Rancho Lobo started calling that night "The Night the Devil Broke Loose," and that name stayed in the memory of a lot of Texas folks, even to this day, partly because of what followed it.

That night took an additional twist for the worse for Chuck Curtin, as some horse thief, bound for hanging for sure, cut Chigger Boom loose from the small barn and stole away in the night with him.

The Curtin barn, small to begin with, presenting smaller target to the powerful wind, sustained little damage, but it was clear to see that someone had slipped Chigger Boom loose from his stall, along with the bridle reins to handle him and a saddle to ride on.

That day started a long and sustained search by Chuck Curtin for his stallion, Chigger Boom.

Chuck's father spoke first as the search was about to begin, the devastation and ruin evident in much of the area about them, "What's all this gear piled beside your saddle bag, Chuck? You going someplace?"

"I'm going out to bring my horse back, Pa. He's waiting on me, looking for me to hurry up and find him. I think he's getting lonesome."

"You be careful out there, Chuck. I can't go with you. I have too much work to do here, but it's okay for you to go. I know what's working on you, but we have no idea the type of man who stole Chigger Boom."

"Oh, Pa, that kind of man deserves what's coming to him. That I know."

The look in his son's face had said it all for Chuck's father. Out and out it all said confidence here was a two-way road.

The trail, as Chuck suspected it would, went away from the ranch in a direct northerly direction and died out almost as soon as it started. The horse thief was obviously dependent upon the storm to hide his tracks. He was right, of course, but Chuck Curtin had thought about the situation at a significant length. He had studied the land and all its characteristics and discounted certain routes of escape and promised he'd check out all others no matter how long it took him. Pursuit, his kind of pursuit, would leave no trace unturned and no chance not looked at. That's why his saddle bag was filled with the necessities for a long trail ride. And other than what he carried, he could live off the land, or find sustenance as providence might supply.

The Saffron Hills were out in front of him, almost due north. The hills were a conglomeration of canyons, caves, narrow passes, and natural culverts that provided water release from small tarns in the higher cliffs. Tree lines came and went at the sign of earth ravage thousands of years earlier where rocky outburst and promontories came from deep eruptions.

The ride was a difficult one, his eyes always looking for a special sign in horse tracks. He found some tracks on crossing trails here and there, but none he was looking for. He was on the search for over a week. On two different occasions he had meals with mountain men who were on their way down to a town or on the way back. They were very solicitous of a lad looking for his horse.

"How'll you find the right track, son?" one old trapper said as they sat before a late fire shooting the breeze. "That corker of a storm even raised the devil up here in the mountains. I damned near didn't sleep the whole night through in my cave, the whole mountain sitting up as my umbrella. Only place to be in a storm like that one, deep inside."

"I fixed it so I could find the track my horse would leave."

The trapper, who called himself Jigger George, over which they had a good laugh, nodded. "Like you had worries before they came on you about this here animal you call Chigger Boom. That's about the strangest name I ever heard for a horse, but of course I'm guessing at that. It's different though. Like maybe it is up there in the high mountains and it's just up to you and your critter and the cool air."

He stopped talking practically in mid-sentence, and said, "You got yourself all prepared for what might come, like looking upstream on yourself and your horse and the mean sons a bitches you run into every now and then. That's good on you, son. I had a dog I loved once, my last one, and believe it or not I called him Pal-O-Mine. Just like it sounds. Lost

100

him on one half of a mountain. He'd a found me, that old Pal-O-Mine, if he was able to scramble, but I guess something got him. Bear or wolf or wild peccary at full hunger. Mean they is, so you keep all them critters to mind. It pays you in the end."

With Chuck taking a first watch at the open fire, Jigger George was sound asleep in five minutes.

Later the next afternoon, well after Jigger George started back on his own trail, Chuck caught his breath under the lee of an overhanging cliff. The mountain rose like a palisade straight up making him dizzy to look up, which he did, hoping when he looked back at the ground he'd see what he thought he saw. The core of excitement was lit up inside him and he wanted to believe everything good around him, including what he thought he had seen on the ground.

Yes. There on the small piece of gravel and loam mix, the way you see a lone star sitting in the dark sky, was the marked shoe of his stallion Chigger Boom. His mount wanted to slip into the shade of the cliff and Chuck pulled him up short, wanting to make sure of the marking, not let it get distorted in any manner.

He hobbled his horse on a loose rock on the canyon floor after sliding off the saddle to check the sign closer.

It was Chigger Boom's right rear shoe, with one shoe nail in a different spot than usual, where Chuck had positioned it himself. His breath caught up in his throat and acceptance sounded in his chest with a pleasant thrill. Up the canyon he looked and saw nothing, and noted the solid rock floor that Chigger Boom must have used passing through this way. But he had found the sign after this long search. The longing for his stallion mushroomed in him, and he remounted.

But portents abounded that day for Chuck Curtin, and it may be argued that he did not see them in his anxiety and excitement of getting near his stallion after a long search. Sight and sense may be interchangeable in one sector, but may also be disparate in another. Though he didn't see anything, he might have sensed something, about himself or his surroundings.

The differences were working on him, as was foreboding, for Chuck Curtin did not know that this day he would kill a man for the first time.

As he started out of the canyon, away from the overhang, he suddenly caught himself, and began thinking out loud: "You're rushing now, Chuck boy, rushing too fast. You found the sign you were looking for, so don't rush without thinking. It's late. They, whoever they are, or him, whoever he is, are not going much further on this day. They too have to pull up and sit down for rest. Just get some rest yourself, and get a start ahead of them in the morning. They have not found out about the shoe, so

101

that looks like it will lead you right to Chigger Boom. Pack it in for the night, and rest this new mount of yours … he's brought you this far in your search."

He unpacked his gear, tied his horse off on a rock, and set about lighting a small fire. Heated coffee lifted its aroma and he ate a biscuit and a piece of dried meat heated in the fire, and set up his bed on saddle and blanket with his weapons near.

It took him a long time to get set for sleep, as it evaded him many times thinking about finding his horse. The fire dwindled down, a bare ember the final sign of its heat, and a single star showed itself over the ridge of the mountain wall opposite him. A mixture of contentment and excitement rearranged their forces within him and he felt the sleep at last begin to descend upon him. He closed his eyes against that lone star and let his body relax.

The single sound he heard, a loose pebble, a small stone dislodged from some position, brought him stiff on his blanket. The rifle, without any effort, came up in his hand and he rolled away from his bed as silently as he could. He heard another sound, like a boot scraping on a stone surface. His horse snickered and a hoarse whisper, born of darkness, settled into his hearing, as it said, "Shush, boy."

His horse was a slight way down the canyon from where Chuck flattened on the canyon floor. He could picture the intruder with his hand, as kindly as possible, settling on the horse's snout. The horse snickered once more and a hoof touched at a hard surface as he must have shifted his weight. The "Shush" came again, not quite as cautious as before, as though its rider, bedded for the night, was still asleep and had not heard any noise.

Chuck heard the slight click of a weapon as though a trigger was set, a safety released. Darkness leaned on everything, the whole night swallowed up.

It was providence then, that in a simple flicker of a last spark from the last ember of the fire, coupling with the light of a lone star overhead, that Chuck Curtin saw a dim shadow within shadows creeping near him. Chuck shifted his rifle into position, the sound sending a sense of danger back at the intruder, and the intruder swung his weapon into position where he thought Chuck was still on the ground. Chuck Curtin fired his rifle at a man for the first time in his life. The man screamed as the shot hit him, and in turn his weapon was fired. The bullet ricocheted harmlessly off the palisade. The next sound was the gurgle of blood in the man's throat and mouth as blood spilled from him.

"We knew you were on our trail, kid. We seen you two days ago, but thought we'd lose you."

"Where's my horse? Who's got him? Where's he headed?"

"I guess I can't hurt anymore, kid. My boss took that horse of yours. Loved him from the first time he saw him one night we went to town." He coughed, spat blood. "I'm going to die, kid. I didn't want any of this, but he's hungry, the boss. Thurman Cosgrove's his name. He's headed for The Gloser Hills. Has a place up there."

He coughed again, the strain wracking his body. "I guess I've paid him all I owed him, from way back. Just don't let them wild pigs get me, kid. I know I can count on you for that. I didn't want any of this. I knew it when we were at your ranch. That was a devil of a night. Some terrible screaming when we came across the prairie like the world was going to end."

He spat again, the pain obviously growing. "I hope you don't ever have to gun somebody else, kid. It hurts on your end, don't it? It did for me the first time. I'm still sorry."

In a twisting spasm that shook his whole body, he moaned again, gurgled again, spat again. The pistol fell to the rocky ground at his side with a sharp click. Out of the whole of night, sounds or silence came either at odds or associated with each other. A wolf howled from some dark recess elsewhere in the mountain range while Chuck's horse snickered. And overhead a shooting star was silent in its sweeping trajectory, as if balancing all of life.

Chuck Curtin, caught up in the moment, said, "What's your name?" He still held the rifle in his hands, waiting for an answer.

There was no response. The man's name stayed with him, and Chuck Curtin buried man and name under a pile of rocks and stones. On a stake planted in the pile, Chuck Curtin scratched a message. It read, "He helped steal Chigger Boom and was sorry."

The young stallion seeker, after saying due words over the body of a stranger, set out after his horse, his target the Cosgrove place in The Gloser Hills, a day's ride away. He hoped that his second killing was not at hand, but he'd do anything to get his horse back.

He rode with intensity tying together all his energies, but at times knew the horse needed his rest too. Water from a stream and dry jerky was Chuck's lunch. The sun was over his right shoulder for the earlier part of the day, and then, after hunger spoke its name at or near mid-day, rested on his back until he stopped to study the foothills leaning upward to The Gloser Hills.

To the end of his days Chuck Curtin swore that Chigger Boom, in a small corral with a rail fence, smelled him on the wind. The stallion snorted and snickered and raised such a clamor among other horses that three men came out of the small cabin to check on the disturbance.

"Hey, Boss," one voice said, "it's that new one you roped in. He

103

must smell a cat out there or a bear or something he don't like."

"Yeh," came a reply that Chuck could hear from his place behind a few trees. "I knew he was special the first time I saw him. We can go back in. It's good he'll let us know if anything gets close to the cabin. He's better than a watch dog. Knew he was special all the way."

The three men went back into the cabin, where a thin plume of smoke with aroma showed a cook stove was working. Darkness deepened and stars came out. A candle flickered in a window, then a lantern glowed and the window turned a pale orange. Once in a while a shadow passed its image across the window.

Later, well after midnight, with the cabin quiet, the lantern shut down, the orange glow gone, Chuck Curtin slipped into the corral and walked straight to Chigger Boom who seemingly stood at attention … horse and beloved master together again, his feeder, his trainer, the one who rubbed him down and kept him healthy, the one who fed him carrots and apples from his hand.

With that reception the three other horses stayed quiet as if under Chigger Boom's spell. Beneath overhead planking Chuck found Chigger Boom's saddle and saddle blanket. He cinched the saddle on the horse, mounted him and slowly lifted the bar at the gate.

Thoughts of the earlier killing came at him. He did not want to repeat that deed. To avoid one he leveled his rifle at the cabin, fired a single round that smashed the window and drove the horses out of the corral. Chigger Boom and his rider went ahead of their rush.

All animals were well out on the prairie before any of the men dared come out of the cabin.

Three days later, after a comfortable and happy ride, Chigger Boom and Chuck Curtin showed up at home. His father had already heard about the burial sign up in a canyon of the Saffron Hills, as had just about everybody in Rancho Lobo.

Many people in the next few years read that last testament for a man. The sign helped carry the tale wherever it was mentioned, in a saloon or barber shop or general store throughout Texas, and all the way to California and Montana and the other territories, about Chigger Boom and the Night the Devil Broke Loose.

Boots and Squeakers

At the Last Good Find Saloon, in Tremont, Texas, two old pards, Josh Madison and Max Kemler, at the end of a hard day, came in off the trail.

A third man, tall, rugged in the face and across the shoulders, early forties, entered the saloon shortly after them, and walked directly to the bar. He wore a wide sombrero, a dark blue vest over a lighter blue shirt, dark pants and no boots or gun belt. His feet were shod with a pair of strange looking "slippers," to use another term.

Madison, a tall cowpoke and strangely neat as a pin, said to his pal, "Hey, Max, who's the gent in the girlie boots?"

Kemler, thinking it over, said, "Reminds me of the lady works the post office in Laramie, Suzie something. 'Member how she hid her feet all the time, the silly looking shoes she wore, like they'd fit a whole horse or even two of them."

Both cowpokes laughed at the memory.

Madison, to the stranger, said, "Hey, mister, how'd you come by those things you got on your feet? Don't you wear a real man's boots like all us others do? Good cowboy boots for wearing working spurs, riding horse, herding cattle? I'd allow you can't put no spurs on them things." He shook his head in anticipation of a silly answer.

The stranger, nodding, broke into a wide grin, looked down at his feet for the longest spell, which seemed to unnerve Madison, and replied, "These things on my feet are my 'squeakers,' as I call them. They make funny sounds when I walk while my real boots are getting fixed by the harness maker down the street. Other than that, my feet are my own concern, son. And so is what I wear on them, on or off a horse."

Madison, suddenly realizing he's been put down, said, "You poking fun at me, Mister? I don't think I like that. What if I was to whip those silly looking things off your feet, them squeakers?"

The stranger, not yet agitated, quietly replied, "Well, son, I expect you'd find one hand broken or one wrist, your tongue hanging out of your mouth more tired than it is right now, and me climbing all over you just for the hell of it. How's that for a sissy-footed cowpoke just looking to please his throat?"

Madison, threatened, finding his own composure breaking down, stood and said, "Hell, mister, I don't like your tone none and you ain't even wearing a gun."

"That's the whole point of it, son," said the stranger. "I ain't wearing a gun, so you can't use yours on me if you had that faulty thought come to your mind, which I observe is busier than it ought to be instead of enjoying your whiskey like you ought. You never know when you might get the taste of the next one. You'll find yourself in jail for at least one night, and maybe more, if you were to pull the trigger on an unarmed man."

Kemler, suddenly seeing what might be coming, cautioned his pal. "Josh, better let it go. Now ain't the time to get this man all riled up. He ain't done nothin' to you."

Madison, still upset, says, "I just don't like his looks, how he talks, how he dresses. He don't look like no cowboy to me."

The barkeep, having heard the whole dialogue, began to tap the bar top like marking time. Finally he said, "Son, pay attention to your pard here, and to the gent you're antagonizin'. It just ain't in your best interest to rile him up and get my place messed up over a pair of funny lookin' feet critters. And he's a whole lot of right by sayin' he'll be all over you in good fashion before you can blow your nose or draw your weapon."

Madison, really agitated, replied, "You think I ain't fast enough to draw and get a bead on him?"

Before Madison could move the stranger slammed a fist in his face, pulled his gun from his holster and trained it on Kemler.

The stranger advised Kemler, "Pick him up real easy, son. Take him outside and dump him in the water trough. Tell him, when he's fully awake, sober as he'll ever be, he can get his gun down at the jail. I'm finishing off my drink now and going back to work. Before I get there, you better get your friend put in one of those cells and make sure the door is locked and the keys hung proper. He's going to be madder than hell later tonight. You must know that, you being his pard."

The stranger walked out of the saloon, the squeakers on his feet making a distinctive noise as he leaves the room. The door closed with another squeak.

Kemler remarked, as he's trying to pick up his pal, "Barkeep, who the hell is that guy? What's his name? What's he do around this here town?"

The barkeep, holding back the easiest smile, offered his answers. "That's Jed Hollander. He's head of the Texas Rangers. One of the real good lawmen in the whole territory. Probably the damnedest best one of all. Tell your pard he don't want him on the other side of anythin'. And if I was you I'd make sure I get that hothead in jail pronto lest he starts to agitatin' the law. Won't pay him to do so."

Kemler, shaking his head, having felt something like this coming his way, said, "Is that man that good? As good as you say?"

The barkeep, glad there's been no fight, offered another answer. "For ten, twelve years he's been between whatever's bad and whatever's good in all this territory, all the way up as far as Plimpton, and you gotta cross the ferry there to get away from him."

Kemler, hustling his friend erect who's shaking his head like he's been kicked by a mule, said, "Is he a married man, this Hollander gent, this Ranger?"

The barkeep, waving his hands like a flagman on the railroad, said, "Whoa, there, son. Why do you ask such a question? You sure don't want to go in that direction. Not if your life was to depend on it. That ain't likely safe from any angle no matter how the hellos go 'twixt who and whoever."

Kemler, smiling sheepishly, gave his answer. "Not me, mister. I'm no lover boy, but Madison here thinks he's the whole shebang to any woman he fancies, and he don't miss much that way either. It's like his getting'-even weapon, if you know what I mean. Seems as though he's been raisin' that kind of hell since he was halfway to the saddle, maybe even 'afore he saw all the sights the barn was holdin' on to. And in the time I been around, that's all the way to Houston and half the ranches in between. Second thought, probably three quarters of 'em. He's like fire and ice, that boy, the miracle worker's what he is. Heats 'em up and leaves 'em cold and him on the trail again. I can't count how many times he's been chased down the trail and the guns goin' off behind him and him laughin' like a damned fool, but smilin' like the ears on his head was really red and black and pointin' the way to Hell itself."

"He leave any kids on the way?" the barkeep wondered aloud.

Kemler, still holding Madison erect, said, "I'd guess half the kids in this part of Texas have that same long clean nose and those deep blue eyes like the whole ocean was here sayin' hello to one girl at a time. He just gets meaner'n Hell if I tell him about them husbands lookin' half the world over for him." He laughed loudly, and continued, "And their women, too."

"Why's he like that?" the bartender asked. "He's a decent lookin' boy."

Kemler thought that point over and said, "My guess is he hates what he can't be. Knows he ain't ever goin' to be a good husband or father or plain law-abidin' son of the west. It just ain't in him for such goodness."

"And you? Why are you like this?"

Kemler said, "I can't be what I want to be either. Simple as that. And that Ranger scares me to Kingdom Come. I should know better."

The barkeep mused, "I'm bettin' he ain't done his bit yet, son. He don't like the bad guys, and 'specially those that play women for trinkets and husbands for fools. The law and most men say women this side of the saloon ain't fair game for any drover comes off the trail like he's the angel itself but ain't."

Kemler carried Madison from the saloon, bound for the jail down the

107

street.

At the jail, with Madison in a cell, young and attractive Alma Hollander, the Ranger's wife, strolled in at noontime carrying a tray of food.

She said to Madison, "I have your lunch here. Please step back and I'll place it on the floor. I'm Mrs. Hollander."

"I know who you are, sweet one," Madison said. "You're the girl who escaped from that bright moon I was studying all last night after I got locked up in here, the one the moon didn't want to let go of, afraid you'd get scooped up by some lovesick cowboy like me who thinks Texas women are the most beautiful women in the whole world, 'specially the married ones. Your husband's a real nice fellow, if he is what he seems to be with someone like you at hand. He does have a great eye for beautiful ladies. How I wish I was not in here, lost to the world, lost to the fairest of ladies in the world."

Alma, turning to exit after placing the tray on the floor, advised him, "Just eat your meal, Madison. That's all you have to do. You'll have your chance someday at true love."

"I just wish it could be you, Ma'am," Madison offered sweetly. "No moss growing all over me. When I move on there'll be some live wishing going on here. You'll just be in the mix then, like a dream that never happened, a beautiful woman locked into a lonely town where the moon can die every night, like death comes on every breath if you let it."

"You are a smooth one, Madison," she said, ready to leave the jail.

Madison, still playing, tried again, "Knowing my name for starters is all it takes. Now let me dream how it might be. I'll let you know how it goes some other time when I'm shuck of here."

Alma is about to leave and Madison snaked his hand through the bars and grabbed her by the hair. He immediately covered her mouth with his other hand and pulled her against the bars of the cell.

Madison, holding tight, whispered in her ear, "That prairie rat of a husband of yours shouldn't let high and mighty you work like a slave. You got some comeuppance coming to you, you and that man of yours who thinks he's the world to you. Well, soft lady, you got some news coming your way."

Madison shifted his position to get a better grab on her, and Hollander stepped into the cell section of the jail.

Hollander, in a deep voice, warned, "You keep your hands on her and you're dead before you hit the floor."

"I got the knife here, high and mighty Ranger, and I'll cut her pretty face so you won't want to look at her come morning any more. I'll mark her fearsome, Ranger boy, real fearsome."

Hollander offered a quick thought on the matter. "She'll probably do what Chico does when she yells at him."

Alma, a quizzical look on her face, imagined her pet dog being corrected, smiled, and then ducked, as Hollander fired one round high onto Madison's shoulder. It knocked Madison across the cell. Alma fell once free of his grip, and the dull knife taken from the food tray dropped harmlessly to the floor.

Hollander added another thought to the matter. "You're going down to the third level at the penitentiary, Madison. You won't see the sun for a few years if you can stand it. I'm willing to wager you'll be nearer to Hell than you are right now."

"And no closer to heaven," Alma Hollander added as she brushed off her clothes.

Hollander laughed all the way out of the jail, even as his "slippers" squeaked again.

ABOUT THE AUTHOR

Tom Sheehan, a 28-time Pushcart Prize nominee, is comfortable writing in several different genres and makes it a point to create each and every day. He's authored the novels *Vigilantes East, Death for the Phantom Receiver, Murder at the Forum* (an NHL novel of Bruins-Canadiens long rivalry), *Death of a Lottery Foe, Death by Punishment, and An Accountable Death,* all available as eBooks. His short story works number *A Collection of Friends, From the Quickening, In the Garden of Long Shadows, Epic Cures,* and *Brief Cases, Short Spans* in all of which he manages to uncannily include a very special character, his hometown of Saugus, Massachusetts. *The Westering*, an eBook, was nominated for a National Book Award. Sheehan's poetic ruminations are *Ah, Devon Unbowed, The Saugus Book, This Rare Earth & Other Flights, Reflections from Vinegar Hill* and the eBook *Korean Echoes*, nominated for a Distinguished Military Award. *Cross Trails* is his third book of western short stories from Pocol Press, the others being *The Nations* and *Where Skies Grow Wide.* Other recognition comes from two Best of the Net Awards for 2015 (*KYSO Flash* and *Right Hand Pointing*) and short story awards in 2013 and 2014 from *Nazar Look*, which also issued his collection, *Six Guns, Inc.,* 2015.

www.ingramcontent.com/pod-product-compliance
Lightning Source LLC
Chambersburg PA
CBHW071133250626
47159CB00006B/2227